HALF-BROKE HEART

COMBAT HEARTS #1.5

TARINA DEATON

Cover Design: Lori LovesBooks Jackson

Editor: Jessica Snyder of www.jessicasnyderedits.com

ALSO BY TARINA DEATON

For the A2T2 Readers.
I can't tell you how much your support has meant.

CHAPTER 1

*D*esire punched Chris in the gut. If sexy had a sound, it would be Denise's laugh. She wiped a finger under her eye as she trailed off in a deep chuckle.

"Chris has a somewhat questionable past," Jase said.

Denise turned off *Magic Mike*, shutting Channing Tatum down mid-hip grind. "Nothing wrong with that."

Grabbing his bag from where he'd dropped it on the floor, Chris raised his eyebrows before following Bree and Jase down the hall to Bree's guest bathroom. Glancing over his shoulder, he watched Denise cross the open living room into the kitchen. Her cut-off shorts were demure by today's standards, ending a few inches below her butt cheeks, but they showcased her long, tanned legs.

Looked like agreeing to go to Bree's for Chinese after camping instead of going home to grilled cheese was going to have more benefits than just the food. He'd been worried he was going to be the uncomfortable third wheel. Now he was uncomfortable for an entirely different reason. He pulled at the front of his cargo pants and shifted his hip a little with his next step.

Bree stopped in the middle of the hall. "There's towels and

normal soap on the counter."

His lips quirked up. "Normal soap?"

"Not perfumey."

He smiled. "Ah. 'Preciate it."

Jase pulled her farther down the hall. "You're welcome," she said over her shoulder.

Chris shut the door and thumbed the lock, dropping his bag on the small wooden stool next to the vanity. Unzipping the bag, he pulled out clean gym shorts and a t-shirt. No underwear. Oh well, he'd just have to keep his mind on innocent topics and off the way those shorts hugged Denise's perfectly formed ass. *Not helping.*

He turned the shower knob all the way to the left and steam filled the room as the water heated. Untying the laces of his boots he kicked them away before pulling his shirt and pants off. He stepped into the shower and ducked his head under the spray, letting the pulsing, hot spray run over his shoulders and back, loosening muscles tight from sleeping in a tent for the last three nights. Not the worst place he'd slept, but definitely not the most comfortable either. He grabbed the bar of soap and worked up a lather, running his hands over his shoulders and chest.

Denise's laugh echoed in his mind, sending blood rushing to his groin. He closed his eyes and tugged on his semi-erection, picturing her long, tan legs wrapped around his hips. *Fuck.*

His eyes snapped open and he released himself. He couldn't rub one out in Bree's shower. Had to get that under control. He lathered up more soap and ran it over his close-cropped hair and three days' worth of beard.

His phone chirped twice in quick succession in his pants pocket. Running his hands over his head one more time, sloughing off the last of the soap, he shut off the water. The towel was soft as he ran it over his body and reminded him he needed to get more laundry detergent. Wrapping it around his waist, he dug in his pants for his phone.

Mtg 0800 Mon
New TF. You're lead.

His gut clenched. If his boss had decided to stand up a new task force, they'd gotten the intelligence they needed. Or shit had gone all to hell. He hoped it was the first option.

DENISE PLACED her glass on the table beside the recliner and sprawled down in the chair. She rubbed her stomach and raised the footrest. "Ugh. I ate too much food."

Bree sat on the end of the couch. "I swear they put something in it that makes it expand after you've eaten it."

Jase joined Bree on the couch. "Lay down with me."

A small pang hit Denise right below her breast bone. She was happy for Bree, seeing her with a guy who obviously cared for her, yet she couldn't help but wonder if she'd ever find something like that. Her service dog, Sprocket, whined and laid her head on the armrest, staring at Denise with her soulful brown eyes. Denise scratched her behind the ear.

Chris flopped down on the other side of the sectional and adjusted the pillow under his head. "Oof." He curled up when Charlie jumped on the couch and landed on top of him.

Bree snapped her fingers. "Charlie, get down."

But Chris wrapped an arm around Charlie's big head and rubbed his ears. "Don't worry about it." His biceps flexed when he pushed the dog to the side, between his body and the back of the couch.

Denise felt another pang—lower this time. Her gaze wandered down his stretched-out body. He raised an arm and rested it under his head, pulling the faded black t-shirt up and exposing a sliver of skin on his abdomen. The intricate full-sleeve tattoo moved as he shifted and flexed.

Her legs twitched, suddenly restless. She'd love to examine his ink further. Not to get close to him, just to see what the tattoo was. She loved what ink said about a person. The story it told. Her own back piece was still a work in progress, only three-quarters finished.

"Denise."

Her eyes refocused, having been mesmerized by the colorful designs. She blinked and looked at Bree. "What?"

"You with us?" Worry lines marred her forehead.

"Yeah. Just digesting."

"Movie?"

She picked up the remote. "Oh, yeah." She flipped through Netflix and queued up *The Expendables* and some hot, ass-kicking Jason Statham.

Fifteen minutes into the movie, low snores rose from both Jase and Chris.

Denise chuckled. "I guess camping takes a lot out of a guy."

"I guess so."

Thirty minutes later, Denise stood and stretched her arms out over her head. "I'm falling asleep, so I'm going to head out."

"Okay, let me untangle myself," Bree said.

"No, stay there. I know where the door is."

"I know, but I'm going to get blankets for them." She lifted Jase's arm from around her waist and rose from the couch. Charlie watched his person stand and raised his head from where it rested on Chris's legs then jumped off the couch. His hind paw landed square in the middle of Chris's crotch, causing him to curl up in a fetal position and groan.

"Son of a bitch," he ground out.

"Oh, shit. Are you okay?" Denise asked.

"Hell, no, I'm not okay. Shit, that burns."

She cringed, but inside was repressing the urge to laugh. "Do you need some ice?"

"What happened?" Jase sat up and ran his hands through his already sleep-tousled hair.

"Charlie unmanned Chris." Bree bit her lip.

"Seems to be a thing in this house." Jase stood and stretched, exposing the bottom of his toned abs. "You ready to go or do you need a minute to retract your ball sac?"

"Screw you," Chris replied.

"I'll pass, thanks for the offer, though."

"I can drop him off once he's recovered enough to walk," Denise offered.

"You sure?" Jase dropped an arm over Bree's shoulders.

She shrugged. "Sure. No reason for you to leave and come back when I'm leaving anyway."

Chris rolled off the couch and landed on his knees, one hand on the floor and the other still cradled around his manhood. Using the couch to brace himself, he stood up but remained hunched over like an old man.

"Shit, that dog has some pointy paws on him. I can't imagine how dangerous he'd be if he had all his legs."

"Just be glad it wasn't Sprocket," Bree said. The large mastiff raised her head.

Chris looked at the dog, still sprawled next to the chair Denise had vacated. "Please tell me you have a truck for that dog and I don't have to try to share a seat with it."

"SUV. She sits in the cargo area," Denise said. Not that it would matter. If her dog wanted to sit in the front, he'd damn well ride in the back.

With a small nod, he hobbled his way to the front door, straightening more with each step until he was mostly upright.

"Thanks for dinner, Bree. Later, asshole." He waved a hand in Jase's direction.

"Later, shithead." He clapped Chris on the back as he passed.

Denise hugged Bree. "It just warms my heart when boys show love and affection for one another." She followed Chris out the door, Sprocket close on her heels.

CHAPTER 2

*T*he night was filled with a cacophony of sound as insects and bullfrogs vied for acoustic supremacy. One frog in particular seemed to have found the tempo of the pain in Chris's groin, its croak keeping time with the throb.

"You doin' okay?"

Humor laced her voice and he glared at her. He hadn't missed her smirk when she'd asked if he needed any ice. Freaking woman had no clue.

"Yeah. I'll survive." He adjusted his gym bag over his shoulder and stayed a few paces behind her. Her hips had a natural sway to them as she walked toward her SUV. He tore his gaze away from her ass.

"It's unlocked." She opened the back hatch of the car. "Up." The giant dog jumped into the cargo section with surprising agility.

He opened the rear passenger door and tossed his bag in the back. The dog rested its head on the top of the seat and licked its chops. He swore it was glaring at him. Hefting himself into the passenger seat, he pulled at the crotch of his shorts.

Denise climbed into the driver's seat and turned the ignition while pulling her seat belt across her chest. The 'V' of her t-shirt dipped low as she snapped the belt into place, showing more than a hint of her ample cleavage.

Get a grip. He ran his hand across his head.

She turned on her GPS. "Where're we going?"

"5339 Old Avalon Drive."

Her fingers flew over the screen while he glanced around the older model SUV. His gaze fixed on the gearshift. "You drive a stick?"

Her thumbs stopped. She looked at him from under her lashes and blinked once. "No." Her face was devoid of any emotion.

A slow grin spread across his face. "That was kind of a dumb question, huh?"

"Little bit." She winked and propped the GPS on top of the dash.

"Sorry. Not used to seeing a manual."

"That's one of the reasons I won't trade it in." She released the parking brake and pulled away from the curb. "The sticker price on a newer model with a standard transmission is ridiculous." She glanced over her shoulder. "Sprocket, lay down."

He looked over his shoulder at the dog whose head obstructed most of the view out the back window. It disappeared behind the seat with a groan.

"What kind of dog is she? He?"

"She. She's an English Mastiff mix. Not sure what she's mixed with though."

"Horse?"

A soft, deep chuckle. "I had the same thought when she kept getting bigger."

"How long have you had her?"

Her hand loosely gripped the knob of the gear shift as she changed gears. The sleeve of her t-shirt hugged the contour of her arm muscles, hinting at a partial tattoo sleeve. "About four years."

"Did you adopt her?"

Fine tension seemed to vibrate through her and she didn't

look at him as she ease to a stop at a red light. "She was given to me through a program I took part in." She stared out the windshield and drummed her thumb on the steering wheel. "Sprocket's a PTSD service dog."

"Oh." A couple of his buddies had PTSD dogs. The change he'd seen in them from before they had their dogs to after had been astounding. He wouldn't have guessed Denise needed a service dog, but he'd only just met her. "You don't put her in a vest?" All his friends' dogs had worn vests identifying them as service animals.

The light changed and she shifted, easing into the intersection. "I only put it on her when we're out in public."

He leaned against the passenger door, turning his body toward Denise and glanced toward the back. "Why Sprocket?"

She glanced at him, a bit sheepish. "Fraggle Rock was my favorite show growing up."

His grin was instantaneous. "Really?"

She tore her eyes from the road. "What?"

He shook his head. No way in hell he was going to tell her he thought it was adorable she named her dog after a Muppet. "Nothin'." A smile still tugged at the corner of his mouth. "Am I taking you out of the way?"

"Not too much. It adds about half an hour to my drive."

"Sorry about that. I'd've had Jase drop me off before if I'd known he was going to stay, but Chinese sounded really good when he asked."

She looked at him again. "It's not a big deal."

"Your significant other won't be upset about you being late?

Her eyebrow arched. "Is that your way of asking if I'm seeing anyone?"

Smooth, dude. He had no skill at all tonight. "Yeah."

Her deep chuckle hit him and the throb in his groin, which had receded, began again for a different reason.

"No. No significant other. You?"

Pulling at the material of his shorts, he shifted in the seat. "Nope."

"Insignificant other?"

"A what?"

"An insignificant other. A fuck buddy."

"Oh. No. Don't have one of those either."

"How come?"

"Why don't I have a fuck buddy?"

"Yeah."

Their conversation had taken an odd turn. How'd they go from him asking if she had a boyfriend to her asking if he had a fuck buddy?

"Uh. Time? Interest? I don't know. Availability?"

Damn. She had a dimple in her right cheek when she smiled wide.

"You're seriously telling me you don't have an availability of women?" She looked at him while she downshifted to turn right.

"For a long-term arrangement? No. Hook-ups? Sure. But that's not what you asked." He couldn't think of any other time he'd had such a candid conversation with a woman. "What about you?"

She shook her head. "No insignificant other. No hook-ups."

He threw her question back at her. "You're telling me you don't have an availability of men?"

Her smile turned sardonic. "Ninety percent of the men in my life are of the four-legged variety."

He doubted that. Denise was sexy as hell. Add witty and a droll sense of humor on top of that and he'd bet good money guys hit on her all the time.

He played with the seatbelt across his chest. "Jase said you run a dog rescue."

"I do. What about you?"

"No dogs."

His reward for deliberately misunderstanding her question was another smile and glimpse of her dimple. "What do you do?"

"FBI."

"Agent or support?"

"Agent."

"Huh. What made you choose the FBI?"

"Did six years in the Army and decided I wanted to be a lawyer."

She threw him a confused look. "But you're not a lawyer."

"Hell, no. That shit was boring as fuck."

Another deep, sultry laugh. Jesus, Mary and Joseph. She should do voice-overs. For porn.

"What about your questionable past?"

"My what?" He'd lost track of the conversation.

"Jase said you had a somewhat questionable past when you guys got to Bree's."

"Oh, that."

"Yes, that."

"College was expensive."

"Yeah."

"The GI Bill took care of most of it, but if I wanted to eat more than ramen noodles I had to work. I bounced and bartended for a while, but between school and the late hours I was exhausted."

She turned into his subdivision. "Okay."

"A guy I had a couple of classes with was prior service and seemed to be rolling in dough. I thought he was dealing."

"Really?"

"Yeah. I finally asked him about it."

"To deal?" Her voice rose with disbelief and she whipped her head around to stare at him.

"No. My curiosity finally got the best of me and I asked if his family was rich."

"Oh." Her shoulders relaxed a little. "And?"

"He was stripping."

"Really?" The humor was back in her voice.

"Yeah. He told me about auditions they were having and the rest is history."

"There's got to be more to it than 'the rest is history.'"

"Let's just say I had enough ones stuffed down my pants on a Friday and Saturday night that I didn't have to work the rest of the week. I graduated top five percent of my class."

She laughed as she made the left onto his street.

"I bet you have some juicy stories."

He did, but he wasn't about to share any of them with her. "Let's just say you women are handsy."

Damn, he'd never reacted so much to a woman's laugh before. It was as if the hair on his body was tuned to the exact frequency of her chuckle.

"Which one? I can't see the house numbers."

He thought about telling her she'd missed it and to drive around the block, just to spend an extra five minutes with her. "Next house on the left. Black pickup in the drive."

She was different than any woman he'd met before, equal parts one-of-the-guys and hottie-next-door. He couldn't decide if he should punch her on the shoulder or ask her to sit on his face.

Pulling in behind his truck, she put the SUV in neutral and set the brake.

They spoke at the same time.

"Is it okay if I—?"

"Do you want to—?"

"You first," she said.

"I was going to ask if you wanted to come in." He had no idea why he invited her in. His dick pulsed in his pants, calling him out for the liar he was. He wanted her to sit on his face—that's why he invited her in.

"Oh, good. Because I need to use your restroom."

Maybe it was her excuse to get in the door. "I reserve the right to check it first, but sure." He got out, grabbed his bag from the backseat, and made his way to the door. Inserting his key in the lock, he felt her presence on his right.

"No Sprocket?" He pushed open the door and flipped on the light.

"She'll be fine for a few minutes in the car."

He dropped his keys on the table by the door and gestured. "Living room, dining room, kitchen." He gestured to each as he pointed them out.

She stood right behind him when he turned, her gaze flicking to his mouth before looking back up again. "Bathroom?"

Her voice was husky, reminding him of the actress who did the voice for Jessica Rabbit. She'd slid her hands into the back pocket of her shorts and her t-shirt stretched across her chest.

Eyes up.

"Let me check it. Pretty sure the seat's up."

Her lips twitched. "Sure."

Turning on the lights as he went, he slipped into the bathroom. The shower needed to be cleaned so he pulled the curtain closed. He flipped the seat down then picked up the boxer shorts from the corner and shoved them into the laundry bag hanging on the back of the door.

Denise waited at the top of the hall.

"Good to go." He stepped out of the doorway and swept his arm out.

"Thanks." She brushed past him and closed the door.

An idea niggled the back of his brain. Not a good one. It was probably going to end up in the *epic fail* column.

He smirked. He'd never not done something just because it was a bad idea.

CHAPTER 3

$\mathcal{T}$he hall light was off when Denise left the bathroom and she paused in the dim hallway.

She wanted to linger. Hang out. Have a beer. Flirt even.

It'd been so long since she'd been attracted to someone—since she'd allowed herself to be attracted to someone—she wasn't sure she could flirt without being a total spaz.

She hadn't been kidding when she said most of the guys in her life had four legs. The others either fell into the friends, family, or employee categories.

She shook her head. Who was she kidding? She was going to go home and curl up with a book, a glass of wine, and Sprocket. Anything else was a bad idea.

Chris had turned off the overhead light and switched on the two table lamps. He stood behind a ladder back chair that he'd put in the center of the living room.

She raised her eyebrows, silently asking the question.

"Want to see a better example of my questionable past?"

Bad idea. Bad idea. Her self-preservation alarm blared full force in her mind.

He tapped his fingers against the back of the chair, all but double-dog daring her to take a seat.

She ignored the warning her mind was desperately sounding. Time to take a chance. "No picking me up and spinning me around. I'm still digesting."

He grinned. "Deal. Have a seat."

Taking the three steps, she sat and placed her hands on her upper thighs. "What brought this on?"

He fiddled with the entertainment center. "You looked disappointed when I wouldn't share any juicy details."

"Did I? Hmm...I don't remember that." She hadn't been disappointed. She'd had no desire to hear about him and the mass of groupies she was sure he'd acquired. Nor had she wanted to explore the reasons why she was opposed to hearing about it.

The first strings and electric notes of Sail by AWOLNATION came from the speakers. "Yup. You got twitchy, right around the corner of your eye." He touched the corner of his eye and strutted toward her.

"I don't get twitchy."

"Squinty then?"

"Not sure that's any better." Her hands slipped down to grip the sides of the chair and she forced herself to drum them on the underside. It was either that or white-knuckle the edges with nervousness, unsure if she should be doing something other than sitting there.

The music hit the heavy electronic beat and throbbed in time to her pounding heart. Chris dropped to his knees, spread them wide and thrust his hips. He went up on one knee and slid across the floor on each subsequent beat like a male Russian ballerina.

What were male ballerinas called? Ballerinos?

Hello! Focus! He whipped his shirt off over his head, revealing a wide chest covered in dark ink and chiseled abs. Liquid warmth coalesced right below her belly button and flowed south. Holy...

wow. She wanted to quote Emma Stone in *Crazy, Stupid, Love* and ask if he was photoshopped.

Tossing his shirt somewhere over his head, his palms covered her knees and he spread them apart. His face lingered inches from the juncture of her thighs.

Heat pooled where she imagined she could feel his breath. Trying not to gasp, she inhaled sharply through her nose. She didn't know what she'd expected—maybe some cheesy version of the Chippendales, but this was more than she'd bargained for. Her fight or flight response kicked in and she fought the urge to jump up and either head for the door or jump Chris.

Using her legs as leverage, he hovered over her as he rose. He spun twice and stopped in perfect time to the music. Dropping into a backward roll, he came up on his forearms, legs slightly akimbo above him.

"Whoa." He dropped onto his stomach. "Whoops. Been a while since I did that move. Should probably practice it more."

If this was what he could do with his body without practice, there'd need to be a national advisory if he started. No wonder he'd been able to put himself through school.

"What's your signature move?" What was she doing? It was as if her long-dormant libido had taken control of her mouth when what she needed to do was tell him goodnight, thanks for the show, so sorry, gotta go.

He paused mid hip thrust. "Hmm...I don't know if I can do that anymore."

"Give it a shot." Bad as it might sound, she needed him to fall on his face to break the mood.

"I hear a challenge."

"If that's what gets you motivated."

Dropping to his knees in front of her again, his hands ran down the outside of her legs from hip to knee.

Shit, this might not go as planned.

He pressed her legs together. "Keep 'em closed." He winked.

"That's what she said." Damn her knee-jerk reaction to an innuendo.

He snorted then stood and spun so his back faced her. He shook his butt, stepping back until he straddled her legs and the chair. Bending at the waist, he braced his hands on the floor before lifting one leg onto the back of her chair and then the other, caging her head between his thighs.

She had a face full of crotch.

Please, god, don't let him fart.

Once the first giggle escaped, she couldn't stop the ones that followed. With nowhere appropriate to put her hands, she tapped the outside of his thigh.

The denim of his jeans brushed against her ears when he rolled forward. The muscles on his back flexed and pulled when he propped his elbows on his knees and twisted to look at her over his shoulder.

"Not the reaction I'm used to getting."

She waved a hand in front of her face, trying to catch her breath. "I'm sorry. All I could think was—" Her head fell back and she laughed. One hand on her chest and the other on her stomach, she gasped and raised her head. "Please don't fart."

Covering her face with her hands she bent forward, overcome by her own hilarity. Or nerves. Whichever it was, it had thankfully killed whatever mood had been building. Her guffaws dwindled to the occasional chuckle and she sat back up.

He'd knelt in front of her at some point and his broad, tattooed chest filled her vision when she opened her eyes.

"You done?" He looked pissed.

If she hadn't been inches from him, she might have missed the amusement in his Caribbean blue eyes.

An involuntary giggle escaped before she forced the muscles of her face to assume a serious expression.

She cleared her throat. "Yes."

Firm, warm lips pressed against hers. The tip of his tongue

traced the seam of her lips, sending waves of lust coursing through her.

She followed him up when he stood from his kneeling position. He gripped the back of her head with both hands, trapping her arms at shoulder height. Heat radiated from him and gathered between her legs.

Pulling her closer, he changed the angle of the kiss. Deeper. Hotter. Turning her on more than anyone had in years. Because it'd been years since she'd been kissed by a man. Or aroused. Or held. Or even inclined to let anyone close enough to try.

Yet here she was in the arms of a guy who exuded alpha-male and sex appeal.

Her skin felt too tight, her body suddenly too small to contain the emotions she was feeling. Not only lust and desire but others as well. And if history had proved nothing else, it was that emotions were a dangerous thing to have.

She angled her chin down and tilted her head forward, breaking the seal of their mouths.

He rested his forehead against hers, his warm, harsh breath fanning across her face and drying the moisture on her lips.

Watching his chest rise and fall, she fought to gather her thoughts. She'd lied to Bree when she told her to do everything she would do because she wasn't going to do it.

Not here. Not now.

Unclenching her fingers from the grip they had on Chris's shoulders, she pulled her head back.

"I need to go," she said.

"You sure?" He still hadn't released her.

"Yeah. I—Sprocket's still in the car." Shit. She'd forgotten about her dog. She'd never forgotten about Sprocket or been in a situation where she failed to notice her absence. Not since she'd gotten her.

"We can bring her in."

The possibility of where tonight could lead flitted through her mind. In seconds, she assessed the possible courses of action and discarded each one. No matter the outcome, sex led to emotions and emotions led to nothing but trouble. She wasn't going to take that chance. Not again.

"I don't think that's a good idea."

"Are you worried about Jase and Bree?"

"No." She shook her head. "It's complicated."

"Isn't it always?"

She smiled. "I think it's probably best if I go home tonight."

His hands ran down her back and slid from her waist before he took a small step back. "This wasn't the plan when I invited you in." He grabbed his shirt from the floor and pulled it over his head.

"I kind of figured when you almost fell on your head."

He smirked. "Probably not my finest moment."

"It was definitely the most entertaining thing I've seen in a while." She felt him close behind as she walked to the door. Her heart still pounded in her chest.

Reaching around her, he grabbed the door knob, surrounding her once again. "Denise."

She looked over her shoulder, afraid if she turned the whole way around she'd lose her will power and climb him like a tree.

"Thanks for the ride." He kissed her cheek, close to her lips, his bottom lip teasing the corner of her mouth.

She ignored the whoosh of sensation that traveled the length of her body. "You're welcome."

He opened the door for her and stood in the threshold while she walked to her SUV, doing her best to ignore the heavy weight of his gaze. She let Sprocket out of the cargo area and into the backseat.

Getting in, she finally looked at Chris. Wide-legged stance, shoulders relaxed, hands in his pockets. Even just standing perfectly still, a slight smirk on his face, he had a bad-ass aura.

Fuck, she was an idiot. The problem was, she didn't know if it was because she should've stayed or because she never should have agreed to sit in that damn chair to begin with.

Sprocket pushed her muzzle against her neck. "I know." She scratched her behind the ear and started the car. "Mommy's making bad decisions again."

CHAPTER 4

*C*hris checked his phone for what felt like the hundredth time since Sunday night. No pings. No texts. No calls.

"Hot date?" his partner, Phil asked.

He glanced up from his phone. "What?"

"That's the tenth time you've checked your phone since lunch. And since it's not your work phone, I have to assume you're waiting for a girl to call you."

"Sorry, man. No hot date." Pulling up another report on his computer screen, he tried to concentrate on the new intelligence they'd received.

"Come on. Give this old married guy a break. I need to live vicariously through someone."

"Dude. You're two years older than I am."

"Yeah, but I've been married to Becca for fifteen years. We schedule sex just to make sure we remember how to do it."

Chris shook his head, not even trying to hide his grin. Phil and his wife were that couple people loved to hate because they were just that cute together. He also knew it wasn't just for show since he'd had the misfortune of picking up Phil's phone one day and

Becca had launched into a description of what she *wasn't* wearing before he could tell her he wasn't Phil.

"If there's no hot date, what's the story?" Phil asked.

Chris sat back in his chair and threw the pen he'd been spinning onto the desk. "I don't know. We hit it off, but she ran. Haven't heard from her since."

"First time for everything."

"What do you mean?"

"You're usually the one ducking calls and texts from chicks until they give up and go away."

Shit. Was that what Denise was doing? Had he totally misread the situation the other night?

No. She'd been into it. He didn't know why she put a halt to things, but he didn't think blowing him off was the reason.

Although she hadn't returned his texts either.

"That's not going to work," he said. "Our best friends are hooking up, so we're going to see each other again one way or another."

"Then I guess you've got two options."

"What would those be, wise old man of relationships?"

"One, shrug it off. Don't act like you've been mooning over her—"

"I'm not mooning."

"*And* be polite when you're in the same place because of your friends."

"And two?"

"And two..." Phil smirked. "Show up at her door and ask her what the hell." He pointed a finger at him. "But don't be a stalker about it."

Option two it was.

"That'll be fifty dollars for the consultation."

"Add it to my bill."

"Shit. If you ever pay your bill all three of my kids'll go to college free and clear."

"We'll just call it the Christopher Nolton scholarship fund."

"Pfft." Phil went back to reading his own reports, weeding through the information in preparation for their meeting with the division chief the next afternoon.

At five o'clock, Phil loosened his tie and groaned. "We good for tomorrow?"

Chris released his own tie from the choke-hold around his neck. "Yeah, we're good. I'll finish the brief tomorrow after we meet with the rest of team so we can give the chief the whole picture."

"Sounds good. I need to go. Phee has a gymnastics meet tonight and I need to fight traffic across town."

"Tell her I said good luck."

Phil punched at the lower corner of his computer screen, turning it off. "I'm not telling her that. That girl doesn't need any more luck. If she places tonight, which is damn near guaranteed, I have to foot the bill for another damn leotard." He stood and shoved his chair under the desk. "Three hundred dollars for a piece of elastic that doesn't even cover my fourteen-year-old's butt."

He snatched his coat from the back of his chair, shrugging into it. "I'm an FBI agent. Why the hell am I talking about leotards?"

"Because you have three talented daughters?" The question was rhetorical. Phil's oldest daughter, Phoebe, already had colleges and Olympic coaches scouting her. Phil was extremely proud of his girls.

"Don't even get me started on Fillipa's dance costumes."

Chris pressed his lips together. "Wouldn't dream of it."

"See you tomorrow." Phil waved over his shoulder, still muttering about the cost of spandex.

Chris grinned and shut down his computer, the blank screen of his cell phone mocking him from his desk. Screw it. She'd mentioned she lived in an apartment at the rescue she ran. Least she could do was tell him no in person.

~

DENISE SANG an off-color jody cadence under her breath as she jogged around the bend in the road. Normally running helped clear her mind, but today it kept going back to how quickly Sarah was deteriorating. She wasn't ready to face the reality of losing one of the two people she was closest to, but it loomed over her like a dark coastal storm, ominous and stifling.

The Wiggle Butt entrance came into view a quarter mile down the straight stretch of county road. The dogs she was running sensed they were close to the end and tried to pick up their speed, pulling her out of her morose thoughts once again. Telling them to heel, she slowed to bring them back by her side. She maintained her normal nine-minute pace until they reached the top of the drive.

Telling them to heel once more, she slowed to a walk and propped her hands on her hips, watching the toes of her shoes as they ambled up the road. The dog on her right pulled at the lead. "*Nein.*" She pulled back on the leash. "*Fuss.*"

Looking up, she saw Chris sitting on the bottom steps of the stairs leading up to her apartment. Well damn, he looked good without a shirt on, but in a light-blue button down, opened at the collar to show off the ink on his chest, and a five o'clock shadow. Down right panty-meltingly delicious.

Little flutters started low in her belly. Tiny butterflies she'd thought were long past dead and gone.

She'd already made the decision to text him back after her run. Bree getting called into the police station the night before because of another murder investigation and then her own back-to-back training appointments all day hadn't given her a lot of time to think about what she wanted to say. "Sorry I left your balls blue" seemed a bit presumptuous.

"Hey." It came out breathy since she was still catching her wind from her run.

The younger dog tried to pull again to get to Chris, excited about seeing a new person. *"Nein. Sitz."* The dog whined but sat as she was told.

"Aren't you worried about being cut in half?" he asked.

She looked down at the hands-free waist leash, guessing where his gaze was directed since he hadn't taken off his stylish sunglasses yet. "No. I only use it for the dogs who are already lead-trained."

"Do you take all the dogs running?" His elbows were propped on his knees, his hands relaxed between his spread legs.

Had he come just to talk about the dogs? She pulled a water bottle from the pocket of her waist strap and took a swallow. "Only if a client asks for them to be trained for it or the dog has a lot of energy."

"Can I pet them?"

She was glad he asked. So many people didn't, thinking the dogs were just pets. She unclipped the right lead from her waist and waited until the dog had settled before telling her, *"Frei".*

"German commands?" He scratched the dog behind her ears.

"Yes. It keeps the dogs from getting confused by anyone else trying to give them commands."

"Does it have a name?"

"Sadie."

"What about that one?"

She looked at the dog sitting patiently on her left. "Toothless."

"She doesn't have any teeth?"

His hands stilled when she laughed. "He has teeth. He's named after the dragon in the movie *How To Train Your Dragon.* The client's daughter named him. She said he was all black like Toothless, so her dad went with that name."

"Go to dinner with me."

Her heart skipped a beat and she worked to keep her breathing steady. She stood on a precipice. It would be so easy to take a step back. And safe. Staying in her comfort zone with her dogs and her few close friends. A step forward meant falling into the unknown. Taking a chance and the risk of letting someone into her tightly controlled space, even if it was only for a little while.

"No."

His face tightened and his shoulders hunched forward almost imperceptibly.

"I've already got dinner in the slow cooker, so we'll have to eat here."

He visibly relaxed. "What are you cooking?"

"Buffalo ranch chicken." She unclipped Toothless from her waist and pulled the Velcro fastening apart. "Besides, I can't go out tonight."

"Why not?"

"*Face Off* comes on. Can you bring her?" She tilted her chin to Sadie. "I need to put them in their kennels and feed everyone."

He stood from the stairs and she felt him at her side.

"What's *Face Off*?" He fell into step with her.

"One of two reality shows I watch."

"Is it a mass murder reality show?"

They reached the converted barn and she lifted the latch on the door. "No. You'll see."

He helped her refill the food and water dishes before following her back out of the barn and across the crushed gravel yard to the office.

It was weird taking the stairs up to her apartment at a normal pace instead of two at a time, but she didn't want to appear like she was in a rush or running from him. She was overly conscious that her ass was likely right in his face as she climbed the stairs. Did she have sweat trickling down her back and butt? She should have let him go first.

Unlocking the door, he loomed large at her back as they entered her apartment. She kicked her shoes off next to the door as Sprocket ambled toward them.

"Hey girl." She rubbed her ears, leaning down to let Sprocket sniff her face.

"You don't take her running?" Chris asked. His shoes clunked on the floor behind her.

"God, no. She's the laziest dog in the world. It's an effort to get her to walk down to the mailbox."

She assessed her apartment with a critical eye, considering it from someone else's perspective. The only person who had ever been there for any length of time was Bree. At only eight hundred square feet, it was still more than she needed. The majority of the space was taken up by the kitchen and the bedroom, two areas she hadn't been willing to skimp on.

Glancing over her shoulder, she said, "It's not much, but it's home."

"It's nice." He pushed his sunglasses up on top of his head. "How did you find this place?"

"The property or the apartment?" she asked, walking into the kitchen.

"Both?"

"Bree found the property with the barn already on it. It needed a roof, but the old horse stalls were perfect for what we wanted to do." She opened the fridge and pulled out a large pitcher of filtered water. "When Bree and I decided to start the rescue, I was living in a crappy apartment in Raleigh. We needed an office building and Bree talked me into a two-story structure so we could turn the top into an apartment for me to live in."

She poured two glasses of water then replaced the pitcher. "I need to take a shower. You're welcome to wait out here." She realized there was nowhere else for him to sit. "Well, this is pretty much the only place you can wait for me."

Chris stepped closer to her. "You mean I can't wait in your bedroom?" he asked with a smirk.

"Sorry, no. That's not an option."

He shrugged. "It never hurts to ask."

Oddly disappointed, even though she'd told him no, she pointed out the TV remote and told him to help himself to whatever he wanted to drink. She rushed through her shower, not taking the time to give her hair a full conditioning like she normally did. She pulled on jeans and a v-neck t-shirt, throwing her hair up in a clip.

Chris was flipping through channels when she exited her bedroom, Sprocket close on her heels.

"Are we eating soon? Because it smells delicious," he said, looking over the back of the overstuffed couch.

"Right now. I use collard greens to make the wraps." she asked?

He pushed up from the couch and joined her at the counter. His shirt stretched just a little at the shoulders, pulling at the seams and his arms were encased in the thin cloth. He really needed a larger shirt, but then his physique wouldn't be so nicely showcased.

Her eyes snapped back to his. "But I have tortillas if you'd prefer."

"I can't say I've ever had collard greens that weren't cooked."

"They're not bad." She shrugged and opened the fridge, grabbing the bushel of greens and bowl of coleslaw. "It adds a fresh snap to the chicken and the coleslaw. I'll fix you one with the collard greens and if you don't like it you can switch to a tortilla." She pulled the lid off the slow cooker and the smell of hot sauce wafted out of the pot.

He stuck his nose over the pot and inhaled deeply. "Jesus Christ, woman, that smells good."

"Wait until you taste it." She pulled the chicken breasts out of the pot and shredded them before scraping the pile back in and mixing it with the sauce to keep it moist. Piling chicken and coleslaw onto the collard green leaves, she fixed two wraps for each of them.

He looked at his plate then back at her. "That's all I get?

She smiled at his disbelieving tone. "You can have more." She picked up her plate. "I usually eat on the couch."

"That's good with me."

He followed her once more and when they sat on the small leather loveseat, he took up more than his fair share. She could feel his heat once again, even though he was at least a foot away. A warm, fluttery feeling formed low in her abdomen.

She really needed to get these responses to him under control. Curling her legs under herself she asked, "Do you mind if we watch *Jeopardy?*"

"Your house, your TV."

"Hand me the remote?"

He held the remote in front of his chest instead of handing it to her, making her reach across him to get it. A tiny grin played at the corner of his lips, teasing her with the memory of how they felt against hers. She grabbed the remote lower than she needed to, dragging the pads of her fingers across the top of his hand. He licked his lips and she could see his nipples pebble under his shirt.

She might be out of practice, but she still knew how to play the game. "Thanks," she said before turning to the TV and flipping the channels as if they hadn't been flirting over the remote.

His gaze burned her skin. Glancing at him, she raised her eyebrows. "What?"

He shook his head. "Nothing." He picked up one of the wraps and took a large bite. Closing his eyes, his head fell back and he groaned. "Oh my god," he said around the food in his mouth. "Shit. Do you cook like this all the time?"

"Um…I'll probably eat this for a week."

He took another bite. "No, you won't. You're not going to have any left."

"Why not?"

"Beause I'm going to eat it all. This is so good." He polished off the rest of the first wrap and dug into the second, devouring it before she'd even finished half of her first one. "I can help myself, right?" He didn't bother waiting for an answer, but rose from the loveseat and stalked into the kitchen.

"Yup."

HE WATCHED her while fixing himself another plate. Holy hell, she made some good food. He'd never considered the old adage "a man's heart is through his stomach," but now he understood where it came from. Her apartment suited her—comfortable leather furniture, bookcases filled with an assortment of topics, pictures of friends and family on the walls, but no useless bric-a-brac. Her apartment was...her. No fuss, no nonsense, but there was something about it all that made him want to kick back and stay awhile.

He sat back on the small love seat, closer than he'd been before. She wasn't getting any room to run.

Her phone rang and she looked at the caller ID before answering, shooting him an apologetic glance.

"Hey, sweetie. What's up?"

He didn't think it was a guy. Not a guy he needed to worry about if she was calling him "sweetie" in that tone.

"Okay, can she talk on the phone?" She set her plate on the low table in front of her and unfolded her legs. "Have you eaten?...Do you want me to bring you buffalo chicken or do you want McDonalds?...McDonalds it is...I'll be over soon." She took the phone away from her ear and shifted on the couch so she was partially facing him, cocking her knee up between them. "I need to cut dinner short. My cousin isn't well and her kids haven't eaten anything since lunch at school."

"Is it the flu?" He took the last bite of his wrap.

She toyed with the hem of her shirt. "She has terminal cancer. She's supposed to go into hospice next month, but I think it may be sooner than that."

"I'm sorry to hear that." It sucked to lose someone that way. "How old are her kids?"

"They're nine and eight, but sometimes they seem so much older." She picked up their plates and took them to the kitchen, placing them in the sink.

"How far apart are they?"

"They're Irish twins," she said, unplugging the slow cooker.

He recovered the coleslaw and put it in the fridge. "I don't know what that means."

"They're less than a year apart."

"Oh, wow, really?"

"Yeah." Her tone didn't invite more questions about her young cousins. She'd become more distant in the last few minutes, as if she was closing herself off from him—not looking directly at him and being short with her answers. "Come on, Sprocket, we're going to see K2."

Sprocket lumbered up from her spot on the floor. Denise locked the door while Chris went down the stairs and waited for her at the bottom.

"I'm sorry tonight got cut short, but thanks for dinner." He wished her hair was down. A strand he could tuck behind her ear or brush away from her face, so he had some reason to touch her.

"You're welcome." She angled her body away from him, as if she'd already started walking away. "Thanks for showing up unannounced."

He shoved his hands in his pockets to keep from touching her. He remembered how her breasts felt crushed against his chest and he wanted to feel it again. That and more. "That's what you get for blowing me off."

"I was going to text you tonight. With everything that happened with Bree yesterday and back-to-back appointments today, I didn't have a chance. I wasn't trying to blow you off."

"What happened with Bree?"

"It's kind of a long story, she had to go to the police station yesterday. Jase knows all about it. He can fill you in, but I need to go take care of my cousins." She pointed toward the back of the building where he assumed she kept her car.

Screw it. He was going to touch her. Leaning forward, he gently grasped the back of her arm and kissed the corner of her mouth like he did Sunday night, barely touching his lips to the edge of hers. He felt the shivers run through her as he trailed his fingers down the back of her arm to her hand, squeezing her fingers before releasing her.

"Don't be a stranger," he said. "I'll try not to text stalk you again." He got in his truck and watched as she walked around the back of the building her large dog next to her. Denise rested her hand on top of the dog's head, threading her fingers through the fur. He started his truck and drove home, more determined than ever to figure out the mystery that was Denise Reynolds.

CHAPTER 5

*C*hris caught the foam football, thrown in a perfect spiral at his head. "Have we heard from Andrew or Teresa?"

He and the three other members of the new task force were discussing the situation with the Southern Anarchists, a red-neck motorcycle gang. He refused to call them a club. He had friends in a club, even rode with them sometimes. The SAs ran guns and drugs and were branching out into human trafficking—they were nothing like the guys he knew.

"No," Phil said. "They've been radio silent going on three weeks. They've missed their last two check-ins with their handler."

Stephanie, the newest member of the team, held her hands up for the ball and Chris tossed it to her. "That's not normal, is it?"

"They've missed a scheduled check-in here or there before, but never two in a row," Phil explained.

"Fuck," Darren said. "I got a bad feeling about this whole mess."

Stephanie squeezed the ball. "My source said they got sent on a run to northern Georgia and he hasn't seen or heard from them since."

"Did they mention the run the last time they checked in?" Darren asked.

"It's not in their notes." She threw him the ball.

Chris paced beside the long table in the conference room, both hands behind his neck. He had the same bad feeling Darren did. Stephanie trusted her source, but no source was perfect. It was possible he was playing both sides of the table, selling to the highest bidder. Or passing bad information at the direction of his gang boss. Either way, his gut told him something about the situation was off and Andrew and Teresa were probably dead. He didn't voice his opinion, although he and Phil shared a few concerned looks.

"What about the rumors Eddie Perry might be granted parole? How is that going to impact the dynamics in the gang?" Darren asked.

"Good question," Chris said, motioning for the ball. He squeezed it and tossed it between his hands while he paced. "Could lead to a power struggle. Make it easier for us to break them up."

"Who's Eddie Perry again? I'm still learning all the major players," Stephanie said.

"You probably would have only come across his name in passing. He was the former VP of the SAs. Sent to jail way before your time," Phil said.

"What'd he go away for?"

"Manslaughter. Beat a good Samaritan to death when he tried to help Eddie's former wife get away from him at a gas station," Chris said.

"Who's the wife? Is she a resource we can tap?" she asked.

Phil flipped through a file on the table. "Sarah Reed. She lives in Fayetteville with her two kids. She's a damn kindergarten teacher."

"How the hell did she hook up with a guy like Eddie Perry?" Darren asked.

Phil thumbed through some more pages. "Doesn't say."

"At least we'll have some leverage with the kids if Eddie gets paroled," Stephanie said.

That train of thought didn't sit right with Chris at all. "Since when do we use kids as leverage?"

"We don't." Chris turned as his section chief, Richard Dickson, entered the conference room. "The kids are off limits."

Stephanie had the sense to backtrack. "I didn't mean use them as bait or anything."

"We aren't using them at all," he said. He glared at Stephanie for a several more seconds before giving his attention to Chris. "Nolton, the Director's looking over the brief you sent up. If she approves it, we're going to send you in."

He stilled. "Undercover?"

"Yes. Your cover will be you're Dillon's brother and looking for him since you haven't heard from him. You've got the experience and look."

"Okay. When?"

"She wants to give the team more time to make contact before we send in someone else." He glanced around at the rest of the team. "You'll go in alone this time."

"Understood." He tried to keep the excitement out of his voice. Boots on the ground was one of the things he loved about his job and one of the things he missed most about being a Ranger.

"And quit throwing that god damn football around in the office. I'm sick of replacing wall monitors." He turned sharply and excited the conference room.

"It's foam, boss," Chris called at his retreating back.

"I don't give a shit."

He grinned and caught the ball Darren tossed him.

"Still cracks me up his name is Dick Dickson," Stephanie said.

"Don't let him hear you call him Dick," Phil said. "Last time someone called him that, he flipped a desk. Literally."

Chris's cell pinged in his pocket and he threw the ball to Phil as he pulled the phone out.

Denise: Busy?

Kind of early for a booty call isn't it?

Haha. Need someone to go w/me to get a dog. Both my employees have class & Bree's at work.

"We good with where we are for now?" he asked everyone.

"Another hot date?" Phil asked.

"Don't you have a dance recital to go to?" Chris taunted.

Phil jerked in his chair. "Shit! What time is it?"

"Three-thirty," Darren said.

"Damn it. Yeah, we're good. I gotta go." He gathered up the documents in front of him and rounded the table.

Chris laughed. "I was kidding."

"May the evil gods of procreation bestow quadruplet girls upon you." Phil rushed out the door.

"Okay. Unless you two have anything else, I think we're good."

They gathered up the files strewn across the table and left the conference room. Chris texted Denise when he reached his desk.

I can help.

Thanks. Can you meet me there? I'll probably need to take the dog to the vet after.

Sure.

Thanks. Here's the address.

He pulled up the address on his directions app. **Give me 30 mins.**

Okay

FLIPPING the phone end over end on her leg, Denise watched the house across the street from where she'd parked. Glancing at her phone, she second-guessed texting Chris to help her. Sprocket stuck her nose in her ear and snuffled.

Scratching her dog's ear, she said, "I'm okay. Just nervous. Which is weird. He's just a guy, right? It's not like it's a date. He's helping me pick up a dog. Safety in numbers, right?"

Sprocket licked her chops.

"You're not a lot of help, you know that? Screw it." Shit, her emotions were all over the place, wanting to take a chance on maybe finding what Bree'd found and still wanting to stay safe in her own little world. There was nothing wrong with that. Safe was comfortable. Familiar.

Safe was…safe.

She turned the phone over to tell Chris never mind. Her thumb hovered over the screen before she tossed it in the cup holder.

"Fuck."

Her side mirror showed a truck pulling up behind her. She watched in her review mirror as Chris opened his door and stepped out. Hmm, he did track pants good. The plain, long-sleeved t-shirt he wore hugged the planes of his chest and bulges of his arms. She pictured him without it, dark ink covering his chest.

She was a glutton for fucking punishment.

He stood scanning the neighborhood and she could see the alertness in his body. The slight tensing of muscles. The assessing way he checked both ends of the street. They weren't in the best area of Fayetteville. Actually, they were in one of the crappiest areas of Fayetteville, which was one of the reasons she needed someone to meet her. She wiped her hands on her dark green cargo pants and slid her low profile holster into the side of her waistband.

"Stay," she told Sprocket. She got out of the car and thumbed the lock button on her key fob.

"Thanks for helping. I wasn't sure if you'd be able to get off."

"Told them I had some errands to run." He looked at the house behind them. "Where's the dog?"

"Across the street." She pointed to the rundown, wood-sided duplex where 4x4 beams struggled to hold up the sagging porch roof. No one was outside and there were no cars in front of the house.

His gaze tracked to the side of her hip where she'd tucked her compact SIG. She pulled the hem of her shirt over it. "Ready?"

He nodded but didn't say anything.

Mentally shrugging, she walked across the street and skirted the side of the house.

"You're not going to knock?"

"No," she said, picking her way through the overgrown weeds. "The person who called said no one was home and I should get the dog today."

"Someone just called and said there's a dog, come get it?"

She could hear the doubt in his voice. "Happens all the time, unfortunately. A lot of rescues won't pick up a dog. They want whoever is surrendering it to bring it to them. If someone takes it to the pound and the dog's a bully breed, it's automatically killed."

"How do you know this isn't a set up?" His tone was accusatory.

She stopped and stared at him, incredulous. "A set up for what?"

He glared at her, but didn't seem to have a ready answer so she kept walking. She spied the tan and white dog chained to a post on the other side of the yard as soon as she reached the short, chain-link fence. The dog lay on its side, not moving.

"What's that next to its butt?" Chris asked.

"If I had to guess, I'd say it's her uterus." She lifted the latch on the gate and wrenched it open.

"I'm not a vet, but isn't that supposed to be on the inside of her body?" Disgust was evident in his voice.

"Yup."

"What causes that?"

"There are a few things that can cause it, but I've seen it mostly in dogs that are used as a breeding factory. It's why the person who called said to come get her."

She rounded the dog so she could see her coming, rather than walking up behind her. The dog opened her eyes but barely spared Denise a glance.

"Hey, pretty girl," she said softly as she squatted in front of her. She held her hand in front of the dog's nose, letting her sniff. Her pink tongue licked her hand once.

"There's a sweet girl." She pulled a mesh muzzle from her cargo pocket. "I'm just going to slip this over your nose so neither of us gets hurt, okay?"

The dog didn't resist having the muzzle put on and Denise didn't want to consider whether she was used to being muzzled or if she'd just given up. Neither option was a good one.

"What'ch y'all doin' to that dog?"

Denise stood and faced the woman standing on the porch next door. "Taking her." She moved her hand closer to her gun and felt Chris come to her other side.

The neighbor leaned a hip against the rail and crossed her arms. "You the rescue chick?"

"You the one who called?"

"Yeah. That dog's on death's door and these folks don't give two fucks to Sunday. My nephew said I should give you a call."

"Who's your nephew?"

"Mario Thompson."

The name was familiar, but she couldn't put a face to it.

"He got his dog Bravo from you last year."

She smiled. "Sorry, I'm better at remembering the dogs than the people."

"He said that too. Her litter's under the porch." She walked back into her house without another word.

Denise looked at Chris. "Can you take her to the car while I check the pups?"

He frowned. "Sure."

She helped him unchain and lift the dog in his arms, crooning to her the whole time. Placing her key fob in his hand, she said, "The lift gate button is under your thumb. Press it twice and put her in the cargo area for now."

He nodded and shot her another glare.

What was that about? Shaking her head, she went to find the puppies.

CHAPTER 6

*C*hris laid the dog down on the folded up moving pad in
the back of Denise's SUV and ran his hand over her side.
Rib bones protruded under her short fur. He wasn't sure what he
was more pissed about—the condition of the dog or the risk
Denise took coming to this part of town. He knew for a fact a
major gang called this area theirs and they wouldn't take it well to
have a white chick coming in and stealing a dog. Shit, the dog
now lying in the back of her car was probably part of a dog
fighting ring.

Denise rounded the side of the car, carrying a beat-up card-
board box in her arms. "Take the pups and put them close to her
belly."

He looked in the box and found four, small squirming puppies.
And one not squirming. "How old are they?" Picking up two, he
put them near the mother and watched as they immediately
latched on to start feeding. The dog finally lifted her head and
looked at the puppies.

"Six weeks. Maybe. They shouldn't have been separated from
her yet." Sprocket whined from the backseat. "It's okay, girl. We'll
get them to Doc Abbie soon."

"Who's Doc Abbie?" He put the other two puppies next to the first two.

"The vet that takes care of the dogs at the rescue." She set the box down and slid it all the way to the back.

"What about the other puppy?"

She shook her head, pressing her lips into a tight line. They stepped back and she closed the door. "Thank you for coming out."

"About that."

"About what?"

A dark gray sedan pulled around the corner and rolled by, the driver slowing to a crawl and staring at them as he passed. Now wasn't the time to ream her for putting herself at risk.

"When will you be home?"

Her eyebrows pinched together. "In about an hour or so. Why?"

"I'll meet you there." He went to his truck, unlocking the doors.

"What for?"

Was she serious? "We'll talk about it at your place. Right now we need to get out of this neighborhood before someone stops to ask us what we're doing." He got in his truck and started it, waiting for her to do the same. She rolled her eyes and he gripped the steering wheel to keep from getting out and yelling at her right there.

He'd never understood the whole wanting to spank a woman before, but holy fuckballs, he got it now. Her cavalier attitude to putting herself in a dangerous situation was pissing him the fuck off. She had no fucking clue what could happen to her in this kind of neighborhood.

His anger continued to roil as she pulled away from the curb. He followed her as far as the All American Expressway, then headed to his gym, needing to burn off some of his anger.

⌒

THOSE HAD BETTER BE *her fucking headlights.* He'd been waiting for over an hour for Denise to get home. Having expected her to already be there after he finished at the gym and showered, his anger had come back in full force when she hadn't been waiting and hadn't answered his calls or texts.

He stood from the bottom steps when he heard her footsteps crunching on the crushed gravel. "What the hell took you so long?"

Sprocket sniffed his shoes and climbed the stairs, but Denise stopped on the peripheral of the pool of light cast by the flood-light, partially hidden by the shadows behind her. "Hi, Denise. I thought you'd be back earlier." She'd lowered her voice to make it sound deeper.

She took a half step to her left. "Sorry it took longer than I thought it would, Chris."

She stepped back to the right. "Is everything okay? You look like warmed over shit."

Step to the left. "Why no, Chris. The dog needed emergency surgery which is going to cost a shit load of money and she may not make it anyway. Then I got a call that my cousin was taken to the ER and I had to sit with her kids until my parents got to her house."

Back to the right. "I'm sorry to hear that. Let me be an asshole some other time then." She pushed passed him and climbed the stairs, her footsteps landing heavily on the wooden steps.

Fuck. He scrubbed a hand over his face and followed her up the stairs, catching the door before it shut behind her.

"Chris, it's late and I'm really not in the mood to deal with whatever crawled up your ass."

"Not in the— Do you have any idea the kind of danger you put yourself in today?"

She yanked open the fridge and pulled out a bottle of wine. "What are you talking about?"

"That was one of the worst areas in Fayetteville. Cops don't even go in that area unless they're called in for something major."

"I'm aware of that, which is why I was armed."

"That's another thing. Do you have a permit to carry concealed? Do you even know how to shoot the damn thing?" Her look told him immediately he'd crossed some kind of line.

She set the stemless wine glass down with a thud. Her stare was even, devoid of emotion. She didn't break eye contact as she pulled her gun from her holster, dropped the magazine and racked the slide back, ejecting the cartridge. Snatching the bullet out of the air, she disassembled the slide from the grip without looking at it and slammed the two pieces on the counter next to her wine glass.

"You know absolutely fuck all about me. Just because we made out and had dinner once does not mean you get to storm into my apartment and mansplain shit to me like I'm a fucking idiot."

Fuck. He'd totally fucked up. "Denise—"

"Get out." She poured wine into her glass, refusing to look at him now.

An urgency to fix what he knew he'd just fucked up threatened to overtake him. He took a step toward her, but stopped when Sprocket put herself in his path and growled low in her throat.

Denise stepped back from the counter and looked down at Sprocket, surprise on her face. She closed her eyes and took a deep breath, letting it out slowly. When she spoke again, her voice was softer. Calmer. But no less adamant. "You need to leave. Now."

"Denise—"

She put her hand on Sprocket's neck. "I needed someone with me because it was an unsafe neighborhood and it's better to not be alone. But make no mistake, I can take care of myself and have been doing so for a very long time. The very last thing I need tonight is to assure you I'm not some helpless little lady that doesn't know what the fuck she's doing. So you need to go."

Dread settled low in his stomach like a knot that he knew, no matter how hard he worked at it, wouldn't untie easily. He knew this wasn't some feminine wiles thing to create drama. For one thing, that wasn't her style. For another, something in the way she stood and in the tone of her voice said she was done with him.

Nothing he said at that point would break through the wall he could see her shoring up around herself. A wall he hadn't even realized he'd been chipping away at until that moment. Inherently, he understood time was what he needed to give her, but everything in the center of his being wanted to fight and push against the barriers she was erecting.

He walked backward to the door, not breaking eye contact until he had to. Jogging down the stairs, he stormed to his truck and slammed the door.

"Fuck! Fuck! Fuck!" He slammed his hand against the steering wheel. Christ, he needed to get a grip. Why was this tearing him up so bad? He'd known her all of a week. Not even that. So why the fuck did he feel like he'd just lost something important?

CHAPTER 7

*D*enise walked around the small two-man tent, stretching out the corners and setting the pegs into the ground and trying not to watch Chris talking to Bree. She'd been aware of him from the moment she'd pulled into the campsite. His presence was impossible to ignore, even yards away. Especially when what she wanted to do was drink him in after not seeing or hearing from him in three weeks. Even having told him to go, watching him walk away had left an ache in her chest that was still there.

Jase squatted down next to her as she set the last peg. "I'm worried about her."

She looked over just as Bree laughed and laid her hand on Chris's arm. A flash of jealousy burned through her. Fuck, she had issues. "She's good." She stood and brushed her hands on her jeans.

Jase rose from his squat. "Why'd you guys leave the dogs at the rescue?"

"There's too much going on out here for them." She crossed her arms over her chest and turned so she wasn't facing Chris directly.

"What if she needs Polly while she's out here?"

Denise cocked her head and assessed Jase. She was still angry with him for the stunt he'd pulled with Bree and part of her didn't want to help him at all. But Bree was genuinely happy. Happier than Denise could remember. So she did the adult thing.

"Polly helps Bree because she senses her moods. She touches her to provide her comfort. To bring her back to the moment."

"Okay. And?"

She gave him a small smile. "Jase, you do the same thing."

"What?"

"Jeez. You telling me you're worried about her? That's sensing her mood." She broke it down further. "You touch her all the time. Bree is a touchy-feely kind of person. She leans into your touch and takes comfort from it."

He pushed his hands into the pockets of his jeans. "I didn't realize that's what I was doing."

She smirked. "That's probably not why you were touching her, but that's what she takes from it. Most of the time, anyway."

He rocked back on his heels. "Thanks."

She told herself the hollow feeling in her chest was from the knowledge that her friend finally found a guy that understood her and wanted to keep her happy. But she wasn't about to let Jase off the hook without a warning.

"I'll still feed you to my dogs if you fuck up again."

"Not gonna happen."

"I figured." She turned back to the group of people, avoiding looking at Chris while scanning the rest of the guys. "So is there a plan or are we just going to sit around and drink all weekend?"

"Just tonight. Probably tomorrow."

"So all weekend then?"

He grinned. "Yeah, pretty much. There's fishing and hiking tomorrow, if people want."

"Cool." She forced a smile. "Let's get to it then."

They joined the group standing off to the side of the small fire burning in a good size circle of stones and Jase introduced Cole, Jordan, Matt, and Patrick.

"We doin' a beer hunt?" Matt rolled the bottle in his hand, sloshing the little bit of liquid in the bottom.

"We're hunting bear?" Bree asked.

"Bear's not in season for another five months," Denise said.

"Wow," Paul said. "I'm impressed you know that."

She shrugged. "I still go out with my dad every year."

"In any case, he said beer, not bear," Patrick said.

"What's a beer hunt?" she asked. "And why are we hunting beer instead of drinking it?"

"It's a friendly competition we do when we come out," Jase said. "We stage beer at designated points and record the coordinates. Divide into two-man teams. Try to find as many of the locations as possible."

"What's the winner get?" Bree asked.

"Lots of beer," Chris said.

Denise finally gave him her full attention. "What's the loser get?"

He grinned, but it didn't fully reach his eyes. "Less beer."

His smile, even half-hearted, did things to her. Things that were out of her control and she hated not being able to rein them in. "Did you set out the beer?"

"I did. Wasn't sure you girls were going to be up for it, so I brought extra in the truck," Chris said.

Oh, fuck no. He should have learned his lesson three weeks ago. "I hear a challenge." Denise faced Bree, hands on her hips. "Did you hear a challenge?"

Bree dropped her arm from Jase's back and stood up straight. "I did, in fact, hear a challenge."

"Y'all think you can beat us?" Cole asked.

She shared a look with Bree. They both loved showing up guys who underestimated them. She clapped her hands. "Let's do this. What are the rules?"

"Chris, you got everything in your truck?" Jase asked.

"Yeah. Give me a sec." She fought against watching his ass while he jogged to the edge of the clearing.

"Each team gets a map, a compass, and a list of coordinates." Jase handed out the maps, lists, and V.E.T. Adventures backpacks Chris returned with. "You get an hour to find as many points and beer as you can."

Bree pulled her hair back in a ponytail. "What happens to the beer that isn't found?"

"We get it tomorrow." Matt shrugged. "There are usually a few bottles left out there."

"Cool. Let me get my hat," Bree said. She came back from their tent, her hair pulled through a faded blue ball cap.

"You sure you don't want to join up with a couple of the guys?" Chris asked.

Denise glared at him. Asshole was acting like nothing had happened. Fine. He wanted to play that game, she could, too. She folded her arms across her chest. "I'll bet you ten bucks we come back with more beer than the guys."

Chris matched her stance and smirked at her. "I'll take that bet."

"Yo! We doin' this or what?" Cole asked.

Chris and Denise continued their stare-down for several more seconds. "Ten minutes to plot your points," Chris said, never breaking eye contact.

Denise pivoted and joined Bree, already marking the map. "How many points are there?"

"Six," Bree said. She moved the compass along the map. "Looks like there's about half a mile between each point."

"I think if we start at the farthest point and work back, we'll be able to hit all the points and beat them back."

"We can also leapfrog after we hit the first point. Get our bearings for the next point and one of us go to the next point while the other loads up the beer."

"Good idea," Denise said. "Have you been running?"

Bree tilted her head back and forth. "Ehh…"

"So I'm running?"

Bree laid her head on her shoulder. "I love you."

"Ugh. You're such a sap."

She raised her head. "I know."

"Ladies?" Cole asked.

"What?" Bree asked. "Oh. Yeah. We're ready."

Jase checked his watch. "Okay. I've got sixteen-oh-four. I'll give you till seventeen-oh-five."

"Aww, man. That's so generous, that extra minute," Cole said.

"Ready?" Jase asked.

"Wait," Bree said. "Are the locations marked with anything?"

"Orange tape," Chris said. "Go!"

"Bree." Jase flipped her ponytail over her shoulder. "Be careful."

Denise waited while Bree tipped her hat and they set off at a jog for the edge of the clearing. Once through the brush, they stopped and took their first direction.

"Got a point?" Bree asked.

"Yeah. You good to jog to the first one?"

"Ugh. I hate running." Bree dragged her feet the first few steps but caught up with Denise. "So what's going on with you and Chris?"

Shit, she'd been hoping she wouldn't catch onto that. "What do you mean?"

"Oh, please. You were giving him the side eye all afternoon. And avoiding him. You don't avoid anyone. You were also more snarky than your usual level of snarky."

She shook her head. "We kissed."

"What?" Bree stopped running.

Denise stopped and walked the few steps back to her, grabbed her arm and dragged her along.

"When? Why didn't you say anything?"

She explained about the strip tease and their kiss, then him getting pissed when she went to Fayetteville to get a dog.

"He said what?"

"Would you stop stopping?" Denise checked the compass and map. "You keep doing that and we're going to lose."

"Like hell we are, not after he mansplained that crap to you. No wonder you were bitchy."

"I thought you said I was snarky."

"I was being nice," Bree panted. "Why didn't you say anything?"

It was Denise's turn to stop and stare at Bree. "Are you serious? With everything you've had going on?"

Bree stopped and put her hands on her knees. "You have to quit doing this shit."

"Doing what?"

"Shutting everything off and acting like nothing affects you."

"I'm not like you, Bree. I don't do the touchy-feely shit."

Her friend stood. "You don't have to do touchy-feely to let someone do it for you. Or more importantly, to you."

Denise rolled her eyes and caught a flash of orange tape. "Oh, hey. Orange tape."

Bree followed her to the marked tree and took the bag from her shoulders. "You're not getting off that easy."

"I'm not getting off at all," Denise said.

"Pretty sure that's your problem." Bree put the cans in the backpack and slipped it back on her shoulders. "You got the next point?"

Denise lined up the compass and map, orienting herself in the direction they needed to go. "That way."

Bree fell in behind her. "I think that Jordan guy was there."

She looked over her shoulder at her. "Where?"

"That convoy attack I was in."

"Shit. Really?"

"Yeah."

"Do you think he recognized you?"

"I don't know. I think he was looking at me kind of funny."

"Maybe it's because you're gorgeous and he's jealous of Jase being all over you."

"Ha ha. I don't think that's it."

"What're you going to do?"

"Ignore it if I can."

"I like that plan," Denise said. "It's a good plan. Practical for all kinds of situations."

Bree glared at her. "Not for you, missy."

"We'll see. I'm going to run on ahead. We're going to that large fallen tree directly in front of us. I'll take the next bearing on the other side."

"Okay," Bree panted. "Fuck, I hate running."

Denise picked up her pace, alternating between watching her feet to avoid stepping into any holes and keeping track of the point she was running to. On the other side of the tree, she took her next bearing and checked on Bree. "You good?"

"Yeah," she called. "Go on." She waved her hand over her head.

She threw her a thumbs up and set off, concentrating on the rhythm of her feet hitting the ground, a steady cadence playing in her head. It helped clear her mind and kept it off Chris—the way his long-sleeved thermal had molded to his chest and abs. The way his butt had looked in the faded woodland camo pants.

She almost ran passed the second orange streamer. Yeah…so much for clearing her mind. Snatching the cans from the ground, she jogged back to Bree. "You going to make it?"

Bree turned her back to Denise so she could load the cans. "I need to start jogging again."

"You know when I run."

"I'm not running with you. You go too far. Two miles is my limit."

She zipped the backpack closed. "You gonna suck it up so we don't lose?" Bree groaned but fell in behind her again.

Denise continued to run ahead to each site, then backtrack to drag a protesting Bree behind her. Only once did she have to back track because she missed a point. She talked Bree into running full out for the quarter mile between the last location and camp and they burst out of the woods mere seconds before Cole and Matt. Bree managed to get the backpack off before she collapsed in a sprawl on the ground.

The guys spent some time teasing them about cheating, but it was all in fun. Good food, good music, and good people. She'd missed this kind of camaraderie. She was having a good time for the first time since she could really remember. Not that she didn't have fun with Bree, but having a good time with someone who knew all your secrets was different.

Then Jordan called Bree "Tampax."

CHAPTER 8

*D*enise dropped her head into her hands and pushed her hair back from her forehead. Leaving the dogs had been a mistake, but who the hell saw that coming?

Tilting her head, she watched Jase carry Bree toward their tent and felt a pang deep in her chest. One of too damn many lately. Glad her best friend had found someone who literally had her, she couldn't ignore that tiny kernel of jealousy. She sighed and pushed up from the camp chair. Even knowing Jase would take care of her, she wouldn't be able to rest without checking on her. Bree would do the same—they'd always had each other's six.

Chris stopped her a few yards from where Jase and Bree stood. "Denise—"

"Not right now, Chris." That pang grew into an ache with him standing right beside her. Having what could be embracing in front of her and what could have been standing next to her, might be more than she could handle right at that moment.

"Jase has her." His voice was low and coaxing. His hand curled gently around her elbow..

He didn't get it. Bree had been there for her at the absolute lowest of low points in her entire life. No way was she going to watch Bree relive one of the worst moments of hers and not check on her. Fairy tale romance hero-to-the-rescue, or not.

"I know that, Chris. I'm not an idiot. But I also know that Bree is really fucking raw right now, because I know how fucking raw she was when it happened. So I don't care if God Almighty reaches down with a caring hand, I will still check on my best friend when she's hurting."

"That's not—"

"Chris, let her through," Bree called.

It was impossible to read his look in the dark, but his fingers lingered on her skin before he released her.

Fighting the urge to rub her hand over the spot he'd touched, she joined Bree.

SHE FULLY INTENDED to go to her own tent and try to sleep, but seeing Chris head into the tree line waylaid her plans and she veered off to follow him. His wide shoulders were barely visible in the darkness, the firelight failing to reach them in the trees.

"What the fuck was that?" she hissed.

"Jesus, Denise." He glanced over his shoulder and did a little jig.

Watching his movements, she figured out too late what he'd gone into the trees to do.

Whoops. Oh, well. Wasn't the first guy she'd caught peeing on a tree, but she gave him a few seconds to right himself and turn around.

She launched right into her tirade. "Who the fuck do you think you are to keep me from my best friend?"

He advanced the five steps between them, eating them up in three. "That's not what I was trying to do."

His presence washed over her. Surrounded and engulfed her

and she struggled not to be overcome by it. "Then what were you doing?"

"Trying to apologize."

"Oh." Just like that her anger dissipated. She'd been looking for a fight, needing something to burn off the fucking emotions she was feeling as a byproduct of Bree's upset, but Chris snatched it away from her.

"I'm sorry I got in your face about you going into Fayetteville to get that dog. In my defense, I didn't know your background."

"You knew I was in the Army," she said.

"Yeah. So's the fat fucking POG who works in the radiology clinic. Doesn't mean he knows the pew end of a gun from the other."

She didn't know what to say. An apology was the last thing she'd expected, figuring his alpha-male ego wouldn't have let him admit he'd been wrong about something.

His fingers traced the edge of her collar, sending shivers racing across her skin. "How's the dog?" he asked.

She swallowed hard, trying to work up some moisture in her suddenly dry mouth. "She's good. She made it."

His other hand smoothed across her hip and around her back. "I missed you."

Her scoff was immediate. "You haven't known me long enough to miss me."

"Yeah. Three weeks ago, I'd have said the same thing. Turns out I'd've been wrong, too."

He kissed her.

No. That wasn't right.

He consumed her. Branded her. Showed her with his lips and tongue how he had missed her. There was no space between their bodies. As soon as his mouth touched hers, he'd yanked her against him, pulling her off balance and forcing her arms around him.

He fisted her hair and tilted her head back. His mouth moved to the side of her chin and he nipped her jaw. "All I've been able to think about was that kiss. One. Perfect. Fucking. Kiss." His teeth bit and his tongue licked between each word.

She needed him to stop talking. Stop invading her mind with *what ifs* and *might bes*. She pulled his mouth back to hers, sucking his bottom lip between her teeth.

He let out a groan and shuffled her back.

"Oomph." Her back hit the trunk of a tree, the sharp bark digging in through her shirt. Not that she cared. All her senses were focused on Chris's hand, having found its way under her fleece pull-over, plumping her breast through her bra.

"Touch me, Denise," he ordered against her lips.

She reached under his shirt and ran her fingers over the hard ridges of his stomach. It was hot, the way he took control, telling her what to do. Not a submissive by any means, nor did she have any desire to be in that type of relationship, but being the dominant personality all the time sucked after a while. Men assumed she'd be aggressive in bed. All she wanted was a little bit of rough. A guy who'd pull her hair and—

Chris tightened his fist in her hair and tilted her head back. "Stay with me, Denise."

At the sting, she hissed in a breath through her teeth. Was he a mind reader? "I'm not going anywhere."

"You weren't paying attention." He moved his hand between her legs, the heel of his hand pressing against the seam of her pants.

"My mind wandered." Her head fell back against his hand and she bucked her hips. It had been too long since someone other than her BOB had gotten her off. Years. Not something she was necessarily proud of, but there was a distinct difference in the build-up going on in that small, compact spot between her legs.

He licked the spot on her neck, right below her ear. "To where?'

"Us fucking."

She felt his smile against her skin. "Good place to wander.

A crash in the woods came from their right and they both froze, senses on high alert.

Jordan stumbled into a tree, bounced off, and fell to the ground.

"Fuck." Chris dropped his forehead to hers. "Need to go help my battle buddy."

"Yeah," she whispered. Jesus, she needed to get her shit together. She'd been willing to fuck Chris against a tree in the woods, surrounded by other people.

If a woman comes in the forest, and there's no one to hear it...?

He took her mouth again, hard, before pulling back slightly. "Keep that thought. The one about us fucking. Maybe not tonight, but I'm going to want to discuss it. Soon." One more quick, hard kiss and he was gone.

She shivered at the sudden loss of his heat. The urge to throat punch Jordan warred with a tiny sense of relief that they'd been interrupted. What was it about Chris that made her lose her iron-willed control? Mentally shaking her head, she pulled her hair back from her face and huffed out a breath.

Damn emotions.

CHAPTER 9

*C*hris picked up his phone, his thumb hovering over the screen, and set it back down.

"That's the third time you've done that in the last ten minutes," Phil said, not bothering to glance away from his computer screen "You developing a tic or you trying to find the balls to make a call?"

He glared at his partner. "I know exactly where my balls are. Wanna see 'em?"

"Thanks, but I've got my own to stare at. Becca keeps them in a crystal box, lovingly displayed on our mantle."

Chris chuckled, knowing Phil was full of shit. "I just don't get this woman."

"Same chick from a few weeks ago or a different one?"

"Same one."

"Let me guess, she pulled a Chris Nolton and you don't know how to handle it."

He sat forward in his chair. "What the fuck is a Chris Nolton?"

Phil stopped looking at the computer and gave Chris his full attention. "Dude, you're the best partner I've ever had. I literally trust you with my life. But when it comes to women, you have a pattern."

"Oh, yeah, what's that?"

"You pick up these girls. They're cute, probably spend a lot of time in front of the mirror practicing their duck hunting face and taking pictures of food they'll never eat. You hook up with 'em for a few weeks and then get so freaking bored, you break off all contact until they quit calling."

Well…damn. It wasn't his fault he'd had more intelligent conversations with Phil's nine-year-old. Although…he did pick the women. So it probably was his fault.

Phil mistook his pondering. "Look, man, I'm not saying you're a bad guy or a man-whore. I'm just saying you have a type."

"That's the thing. She doesn't fit into the box you just described. She's completely different from every single woman I've ever dated."

"So grab your balls and call her." Phil turned his attention back to his computer.

Instead of his balls, Chris grabbed his phone from the desk and headed to the hall.

"You're not even going to let me listen?" his partner called out.

Chris flipped him off over his shoulder, the phone already pressed to his ear. Three rings and it went to voice mail.

"This is Denise. Leave a message."

"Hey. It's Chris. Give me a call." He hit the red button as a text bubble popped up.

Can't talk now. Checking my cousin into the hospital.

Shit. Probably not the time to ask her if she was ready to finish their conversation from the camping trip.

Is everything ok?

Not really. What did you need?

Was going to ask if you wanted to get dinner tonight.

Won't be home till after 6.

He took that as a positive sign.

How do you feel about BBQ?

As a condiment or a method of cooking?

He grinned. It probably wasn't healthy that he found her sarcasm so funny.

As a food in general.

I prefer dry rub.

If things went the way he wanted, they'd both be getting something rubbed.

6:30 work? I'll bring food.

Sure.

See you then.

He read back through the texts and thought about what Phil said. Other than the little bit of sarcasm, she didn't prevaricate. Didn't try to pretend she might have other plans, even when she had every excuse to blow him off. She didn't have time or patience for games or bullshit. Maybe that was her biggest draw, other than the obvious reasons—he was sick of the bullshit.

Seeing Jase open up with Bree...he was almost a different person. It made Chris wonder if what they said about the love of a good woman was true.

Fuck. Who said anything about love?

He scratched at the four-day beard he was trying to decide to shave or let grow. He'd let it go another couple of days to make up for all the emotional revelations he was having. If he kept that shit up, he was going to have to surrender his man card. Or put his balls in a crystal box.

A DEEP, loud woof sounded from the other side of the door as Chris waited on the landing. He heard Denise tell Sprocket to sit before she opened the door.

"Hey. Come on in." She stepped back, using her lean, well-defined leg as a barrier for Sprocket.

Following her in, he took in the way her cutoffs showcased her legs. He'd never given any thought to the life of a string hanging off a piece of fabric before, but watching the tattered edges of her shorts brush against the smooth skin of her upper thighs, he had all kinds of thoughts about them.

The bag in his hand rustled and he pulled it away from Sprocket's nose. "Not for you, sorry." He headed for the kitchen and placed the bag and six-pack of beer on the counter. "I remember you said you liked lager, so I brought some from a microbrewery I like."

She stood close to him at the counter, took a bottle from the box, and looked at the label. "When did I tell you I liked lager?"

He scratched at the beard growth under his chin. "I may have overheard you mention it to Matt after the beer chase."

Her gaze lifted to his, then moved to his mouth. She pursed her lips and gave a short, distinct nod, as if she'd just figured something out or come to a decision.

He didn't know how to take her actions. Her face gave nothing away and he'd been trained to read peoples' micro expressions.

She set the bottle back in the carrier, her movements slow and precise. He watched as her chest expanded and contracted with the deep breath she took.

"Sprocket, bed." She watched over her shoulder as her dog lumbered to the large pad in the corner of the living room. Her gaze found his once again and he could finally see some emotion. Her pupils dilated and her nostrils flared, ever so slightly.

Then he was moving backward, her hands on his stomach pushing him back against the refrigerator. His head tilted down as hers reached up, seeking his mouth, and one of her hands went behind his head while the other went under his shirt.

He gripped the firm expanse of her ass, his fingers finding the edge of her shorts as they moved toward the juncture of her thighs. Crouching slightly, he ran his hands along the thick seam of her shorts and pulled at her thighs, giving her no choice but to lift her legs around his waist.

She pulled her mouth from his. "You're not going to be able to —" He hefted her up. "Oh, we're doing this."

Using his hips, he pushed away from the fridge. "Don't challenge me, woman." He strode around the end of the counter, heading to the only other door in her apartment—the one that led to a bed.

"Or what?" One of her eyebrows lifted at the corner.

Damn, she was beautiful. And yeah—challenging. She wasn't going to let him take an inch. He was going to have to fight for everything she gave him.

He grinned. It was going to be fucking worth it. He tossed her down on the bed and she bounced, bracing her hands out to the side.

"I might have to find something creative to do to make you see the error of you ways."

Her legs dangled off the bed and he knelt down between them. Hooking his hands behind her knees, he pulled her close to the edge. How easy was it to rip denim?

She didn't give him the chance to find out as her fingers undid the button of her shorts.

He smacked the tops of her hands and she snatched them away.

"Ow! What the hell was that for?"

"Mine."

Her eyebrows rose to her hairline and her eyes grew wide. "Excuse me?"

Bracing her legs apart, he buried his face between them, using his teeth to scrape the seam of her shorts. "Mine," he growled.

She fell back on the bed. "Yup. All yours. Have at it."

"That's what I thought." He unzipped her shorts before hooking his hands into the waistband and pulling them down her legs, revealing her black and red diamond underwear with a black face mask on them.

"Is this—are you wearing Harley Quinn underwear?"

Denise's head lifted from the bed and she glared down the hills and valleys of her body. "Do not make fun of my girl crush."

He ran a hand over his mouth, knowing he wasn't doing shit to hide his smile. "Wouldn't dream of it."

She continued to give him the evil eye.

"Mind if I leave them on for a few minutes while I let the visual of you and your girl crush simmer in my mind?"

Her lips twitched slightly. "It's your boat. Float it." Her head dropped back to the bed.

Oh, yeah. He could work with that. He ran his nose up the center of her underwear, inhaling the sharp, musky scent of her arousal.

Nipping with his teeth and pushing with the hard tip of his tongue, he took her to the edge of release before backing off. He was surprised by how quickly he got her there and smiled when she growled her frustration. Rising from his position between her legs, he hovered over her upper body, running his nose up the centerline of her body while he pushed her shirt up her torso revealing tendrils of gray and black ink swirling across her ribs and under her right breast.

Curiosity to see what the tattoo was almost diverted him from getting her naked, but it felt like it had taken years to get her there and he wasn't going to stop for anything. He'd take the time to explore her ink later, after he'd gotten his fill of her. And she got filled by him.

Standing straight, he stared down at her. Her gaze, traveling down his body and lingering on his crotch, felt like a physical touch and he wondered what she was thinking.

She arched her back and curved her shoulders up to take off her shirt, tossing it at his head with a smirk. Sitting up, she scooted back on her bed until her feet no longer dangled off it and reached behind her to unhook her bra.

He wet his lips, anticipation racing through him.

"You first," she said, her hands still behind her back.

"But I'm not wearing a bra."

She grinned, her dimple making an appearance. "And I'm not wearing any pants, so lose something."

Fuck that, he lost everything. He couldn't remember the last time he'd shucked his clothes so fast. So fast that he got tangled up in his shoes and fell on his ass.

Her deep, husky laughter filled the quiet and his arousal, already pretty damn epic, ramped up another notch.

She cleared her throat. "You okay?"

"Yup, just doing some pushups to make my muscles stand out." He kicked out of his pants and figuratively kicked himself in the ass. *Smooth move, Don Juan.* Shit, he hadn't been this eager when he'd lost his virginity. He popped up and assumed a super-hero pose—hands fisted on his hips, chest puffed out, and his head tilted up slightly.

She laughed again, falling back on the bed.

He dropped his pose. "Fuck, woman. Your laugh."

"What about it?"

"It's a fucking aphrodisiac. Makes me hard every time I hear it."

A shadow across her eyes and she stopped laughing. "You don't have to do that. I'm not that girl."

He shook his head. "What girl?"

"The hearts and flowers kind of girl. You don't have to feed me a line to make me believe I'm going to be something to you that I'm not."

What the fuck? He crawled over her until his knees were on either side of her hips. Taking one of her hands, he placed it over his cock, pushing against the opening of his boxers. "Does this feel like a line?"

She rubbed her palm up and down the length but didn't say anything.

He bit back a groan and forced himself to finish what he wanted to say. "The first time I heard you laugh, I almost rubbed one out in Bree's shower."

Her eyebrows rose sharply and she pulled her lips between her teeth.

"I don't know who fucked with your head so bad that *you*, of all people, would think I was feeding you a line, but I'm not. I don't know where this thing between us is going. I don't know if it's going to go anywhere at all. But don't ever think you aren't sexy as all hell and that I don't get turned on when you're around. Especially when you and your girl are together and cracking each other up. Now, are there any other questions before we continue with tonight's entertainment?"

Her tongue darted out and she wet her lips. The fire was back in her eyes, thank fuck. "Do you have any condoms? Because I don't."

"Yeah. I need to get it out of my wallet."

"You should probably do that, then."

He leaned down and gave her a hard kiss. "I'm on it. Then I'm on you."

"Oh my god."

He could hear the eye roll in her tone as he leaned over the edge of the bed. When he righted himself, she'd taken off her bra. Her large, dark pink nipples were hard and stood out from the creamy expanse of skin that never saw the sun. "Sweet baby Jesus loves me."

She grinned and shook her head at him.

"I'm getting the sense sex hasn't been very fun for you." He ran his tongue from the edge of her panties, over the small swell of her belly, and up the middle of her torso to the center of her breasts.

"Oh, I've had fun sex. I just don't remember ever having funny sex."

"All sex is funny. Haven't you ever watched porn?"

Her dimple made another appearance and her hands moved up his sides and over his shoulders. "Not recently."

He tweaked her nipples with his fingers and then palmed them, rubbing and massaging them, feeling her breath catch as he squeezed. "Those women should be in the running for the Oscars. Best damn acting you've ever seen."

She moved her hands down his sides and hooked her thumbs into the waistband of his boxers, edging them over his ass and down his upper thighs, reaching as far as she could. Her legs came up on either side of him and she used her toes to push his underwear the rest of the way down his legs.

He kicked out of them and stared down between their bodies. "Nice feat of accomplishment." Looking back at her, he wiggled his eyebrows. "Get it? *Feat?*"

She covered her eyes with one hand and laughed. "Oh my god. That was horrible."

"I seem to be at a disadvantage though."

"How's that?" she asked.

"There seems to be a super-hero blocking my progress."

"She's an anti-hero."

"She's still in the way."

"Then by all means, you should take care of that."

"With pleasure." He eased the cotton panties over her hips and down her legs. He wanted to savor this moment. Revealing her. He'd always been that kid who carefully pulled the tape off birthday and Christmas presents because he knew the anticipation could only last for so long.

He hunched over and licked between the juncture of her legs, finding her sensitive clit through her swollen folds. She arched and hissed in a breath. He'd only meant to have a taste, but she was so responsive he couldn't help but do it again. And again.

She planted her feet on the bed and pressed her hips up against his mouth. "Chris," she panted. "Chris!"

"Yeah?" He pulled back slightly, his hands propped under her hips, keeping her within easy reach.

"I'd like you to fuck me now, please."

"Yes, ma'am." He gave her one last lick and lowered her to the bed. Grabbing the condom he'd set to the side, he ripped the packet open and rolled it down his hard length. Bracing himself on his hands, he lowered his hips to hers and pumped them up and down, running his cock between her slick folds.

Her legs came up around his hips and she pushed against the inside of his elbows, causing them to buckle. "Quit teasing." She pulled his head down to her and kissed him. Reaching between their bodies with her other hand, she grabbed his cock, pumping it twice before guiding it to her entrance.

He pushed forward and was immediately met with her impossibly tight sheath. Fuck. She was so tight, he had to back off and inch forward again. He gritted his teeth, fighting for entrance.

"Fuck. Shit. You're so fucking tight."

She tilted her hips, giving him a better angle and he finally sank into her. He felt her clench around him and he twitched, sinking even further in. "Christ almighty, I'm not going to last if you keep doing that."

"Sorry," she said against his neck. "It's been a while."

He pulled out slowly and eased back in. "How long is a while?" *Shit. Don't ask her that.* Too late now.

"Uh." She met his thrusts, her hands trailing down his back and gripping his ass cheeks. "Seven years or so."

He reared up onto his elbows. "Seven years?" She hadn't had sex in *seven years*? And she picked him to break her streak? Fuck. No pressure or anything.

"I heard if I went ten years, I'd revirginize."

"What? That's not really a thing is it?"

She tilted her head back and laughed. "No, but you were looking at me like I'd grown another head."

He could feel her inner muscles contracting when she laughed. Combined with the sound of it, he didn't care if she had managed revirginization, he was about to send her back to square one. "You know this gives a whole new meaning to the phrase *seven-year itch*, right?"

"Yeah. You mind scratching it for me?"

He grinned down at her. "My pleasure." He surged forward again as he kissed her. Her mouth met his, their tongues dueling, while her hips met his thrusts. One of her legs rose high on his back, opening her up more for him and he groaned, hooking his arm under it to keep it in place.

The tips of her nails scraped through the short hair on the back of his head, not enough to hurt but enough to sting a little. He fisted his other hand at the base of her neck, remembering her reaction when he'd pulled her hair when they made out in the woods.

"God, you feel so good," he said against her lips. "Jesus, the way you're squeezing me." He dropped his head onto the bed next to hers. "Fuck, Denise."

"Harder, Chris." Fingers dug into the soft flesh of his butt, squeezing and releasing to the same rhythm of his thrusts. Her teeth scraped against the sensitive skin behind his ear, right before she sank them into his shoulder and grunted.

Her inner muscles squeezed his cock and he could feel the waves of her orgasm as her whole body clamped down on him.

"Ah, shit." He pulled her hair and heard her neck crack with the force. *Oh, shit.* But he was too far gone to stop and ask if she was okay. His whole body shuddered as he came. Her thighs squeezed tight around his waist as her hips rolled up to meet him.

Muscle by muscle he began to relax, small tremors racing through his body. "Are you okay?"

She rubbed the short hair on the back of his neck. "Yeah." Her legs slowly relaxed from around his waist.

"Are you paralyzed?"

He felt her chuckle. "No, but the tingling in my toes is still a little extreme. And I've got a cramp." She stretched out one of her legs.

Reaching between them, he eased out of her and rolled to the side. "I didn't mean to pull your neck that hard."

"It's alright. It actually feels good. Saves me from having to go to the chiropractor for an adjustment." Her stomach grumbled and they both looked down at it. "You did bring food, right?"

He brushed a strand of hair off her neck and kissed her softly. "Yeah. Meet you in the kitchen?"

CHAPTER 10

"*W*hat?"

Chris stared at her from where he stood between her legs as she sat on the counter, wearing only underwear and his t-shirt while they picked at the barbecue he'd brought.

"You're different when you're not around Bree."

That wasn't what she expected to hear. She thought for sure he was going to bring up her self-imposed exile into celibacy. "How's that?"

"You laugh more when you're around her."

She shrugged, trying not to stare so obviously at his chest. "She's my person. She brings out the best in me."

"Your person?"

"Do you believe in soul mates?"

His look was the picture definition of skeptical. "You mean like love everlasting, fairytales, and all that crap?"

She grinned. "Kind of, but not really. I mean like there are going to be a finite number of people in your life that are going to get you. They may be lovers, they may be the person you marry, they could be older, younger, or they may be your best friend in the whole world. Bree is my person."

He held a piece of rib meat to her lips. She pulled her head back, started at the meat, at him, then back at the meat before taking the bite between her teeth.

"Did you think it was going to bite you back?"

Watching him suck the barbecue from his fingers, she said, "The whole feeding each other is one of those romance-y things couples do." She took a sip of beer from the bottle he'd opened.

He took the bottle from her. "You don't do romance-y things?"

"No." She shook her head and pulled off a piece of meat from the ribs. He grabbed her hand and ate the meat, running his tongue between her fingers and sending a pulse directly to her clit.

"So no flowers or chocolates then?"

She scowled at him and tore another piece off, leaning back as far as she could out of his reach to eat it while he pretended to try to steal it. "You can bring chocolates, as long as they're not in a heart-shaped box, and as long as it's not Hershey's. Flowers for no reason are good, but not on a commercial holiday. Then they're just cliché and an obligation."

"Is there a reason you don't like all the romance-y things?"

She picked up the bottle and tore at the label. How much should she tell him? There were only a few people in the world who knew her whole story and she trusted them implicitly. But that's what it came down to—trust. Could she trust Chris? She'd told Bree to give Jase a chance. No time like the present to take her own advice.

"There was a guy once, who said and did all the right things, back when I took people at face value. None of it was true."

Chris's thumbs caressed her thighs where the shirt hem sat. Anyone else doing that would have set her nerves on edge, but right then, she just wished he'd move his thumbs higher.

"He was married?"

"Among other things." She chugged the remainder of the beer and set the bottle down on the counter, bracing her hands next to her legs, unable to meet his gaze. "He killed someone I cared about."

His hands stilled on her legs, fingers pressing into the flesh of her thighs, and his whole body became rigid.

Sprocket trotted around the corner of the counter and whined. Sitting as close as she could, she licked Denise's calf and rested her chin on the top of her foot. Denise rubbed the underside of the dog's chin. Chris looped his arms around her hips and laced his fingers behind her back.

"I lost my shit. He was sent back to the States and it was all swept under the rug. I applied to the Cultural Support Team and told my command if they didn't approve my transfer, the situation wouldn't stay under the rug. I left for training two months later."

Taking a chance, she peeked at him from under her lashes. Anger and disbelief flashed across his face. She could tell he had so many questions he wanted to ask. His Adam's apple bobbed up and down.

"Is he the reason for your seven-year streak?"

Her heart felt like it double-thumped in her chest, grateful he wasn't going to ask any further questions. She hadn't meant to blurt that out and she didn't know if she was prepared to share the whole story yet. Maybe he could see that. Maybe he was willing to let her tell it in her own time. "Partly. After I left the Army I was…angry…for a long time. It got— I was—" She took a deep breath and blew it out. "I was suicidal."

"What happened?"

"Bree convinced me to check myself into an inpatient treatment facility with the VA."

He pulled her hips closer to the edge of the counter, closing the distance between them. "For how long?"

She traced the whorls and shading of the tattoo on his arm, needing something to do with her hands. Who was she kidding?

She needed to touch him. For the first time in longer than she could remember, she wanted to touch someone intimately and draw comfort from their presence. "I lasted two weeks. My therapist and I agreed it was not the right setting for me."

"Why's that?" His voice was soft. Encouraging. She could count on one hand how many people knew what she'd been through. It helped he knew where she was coming from. He wasn't asking out of some perverse curiosity to hear about the poor veteran suffering from PTSD.

"The group therapy was making me more angry instead of less angry."

"Why did it make you more angry?"

"There were people that had never left their base—never saw direct combat, but they were in the same program I was. I was angry that I was dealing with all that crap and they couldn't handle a little indirect fire." She shook her head. "What I thought wasn't fair, but at the time I couldn't see that. We all have different experiences and deal with things in different ways."

His bright blue eyes shifted between hers. The rough pad of his forefinger traced the small scar high on her temple, then moved down her cheek and across her bottom lip. "What happened after two weeks?"

"We agreed I would do better as an outpatient with daily, one-on-one therapy. I got Sprocket. And Bree didn't leave me the fuck alone for three months."

His smile was quick but sad. Her story wasn't a new one. So many others had been in her position. Were in her position. She was one of the lucky ones.

"Have you had enough to eat?"

She glanced down at the to-go container on the counter. "Yeah, for now. Why?"

"I figure with a seven-year hiatus, you're out of practice."

His biceps were warm and hard under her hands as she ran them up his arms to his shoulders. She wanted to stop talking about her past. It was something she still struggled with, but it wasn't who she wanted to be anymore. Protecting herself hadn't gotten her anywhere but by herself. It was time to take a chance on trusting someone again.

"Hmm. I could be a little rusty I suppose, although I always thought it was like riding a bike."

"True, but even if you remember how to ride a bike, you're still a little wobbly until you find your balance again." He ran his hands down her legs until he reached her knees and wrapped her legs around his hips.

Sprocket huffed and snorted at them, turned her huge body around, and lumbered out of the kitchen. Seemed her dog agreed it was time to do things differently.

"How do you suggest I get my balance back?"

He wedged his hands under her ass and pulled her off the counter, hefting her up to get a tighter hold. "First thing I'm going to do is bend you over the bed and explore that tattoo on your back."

She grinned. "Does that mean I get to explore all your tattoos?"

"Abso-fucking-lutely."

CHAPTER 11

*D*inner?

Denise smiled down at the text and her fingers flew across the screen.

Brunch

What?

I thought we were texting random meals.

LOL. No, can you do dinner tonight?

Oohh. Sorry, taking my cousins out for dinner & a movie.

What about tomorrow?

I can probably fit you in tomorrow. You coming here?

Sure. Don't suppose you want to make that chicken in the slow cooker again?

She pressed her lips together. **I can probably make that happen.**

Awesome. See you tomorrow.

"Who's the guy?" Dr. Tailor asked, coming out of her office.

Denise's head snapped up. "What guy?"

Dr. Tailor smiled her annoying, knowing smile and motioned for Denise to follow her into her office. Even though she was only a few years older than Denise, getting caught texting Chris by

Liana Tailor still felt like she'd been caught by her mom sexting a boy when she was supposed to be doing homework. This was going to be an interesting session. Sprocket huffed at her.

"Don't you start." She pushed up from the chair and followed Dr. Tailor into her office, closing the door behind her. Taking her normal seat on the end of the couch, she kicked off her shoes and folded her legs under her.

Dr. Tailor sat in the chair perpendicular to the end of the couch with her notepad and crossed her legs. "So? Who is he?"

"How do you know I wasn't texting Bree?"

"Because you would have just told me it was Bree if it were."

Damn it! She felt like snapping her fingers and saying *curses*. "He's someone I met through Bree and Jase."

Dr. Tailor consulted her notes, flipping through a few pages. "Is this a friend of Bree or a friend of Jase?"

"Jase." She and Bree had an agreement they could talk about each other with Dr. Tailor, something that made their sessions easier than trying to talk around things.

Dr. Tailor released the pages of her notepad. "Tell me about him."

Denise took a deep breath. "He's...not what I expected."

"How so?"

"Well, he's former Special Forces. Definitely an alpha-male, but at the same time he's funny and doesn't seem to take himself seriously all the time."

"In what way?"

She chewed at the dry cuticle around her thumb. "He can laugh at himself and make fun of himself, but he's got that...something...under the surface that you know he can go right to serious if he needs to." Sprocket hefted herself up on the couch and rested her head on Denise's hip. She scratched the dog behind her ears.

"Why does talking about him make you nervous?"

She glanced at Dr. Tailor, who pointed at Sprocket. Damn dog gave her away to anyone who knew what she did.

"He's everything I swore I would stay away from and..." She shrugged. "I like him."

"And that makes you nervous?"

"Things didn't go so well with the last guy I liked."

"You realize that *he* is not indicative of every man you will ever meet?"

"Intellectually, after many, many years of therapy, yes I realize that. But that stuff in here?" She made a small, uneven circle over the center of her chest. "Not so much."

"So it's your own judgment you don't trust."

"My own judgment didn't serve me so well the last time." Sprocket shifted her head higher against her hip and licked her chops.

"You're a different person now."

"Yeah."

"You don't sound very confident, Denise. That isn't like you at all."

"It's just...if I let myself get involved with him... If I let this be more than sex..." She couldn't finish her thoughts. She wasn't even sure what she was trying to articulate.

"You might feel something for him?" Dr. Tailor prompted.

She pursed her lips together and nodded roughly, staring blankly at the tissue box on the low table in front of the couch.

"Would that be a bad thing?"

"With losing Sarah, I don't know if I have the energy or capacity to add someone else to the mix."

"How is she doing?"

Oh, goody. Something else she didn't want to talk about. Therapy was awesome. "She's in hospice."

"Have her doctors said how much longer she has?"

"Anywhere from six days to six months. It depends on the day. And the doctor. It seems like there's a different prognosis every time I go to see her. The worst part is she's starting to push Kimber and Kaden away. Mom and Dad and I make sure we take them with us as often as we can, but she tires so easily." Her eyes stung and she reached forward for a tissue.

"How are Kimber and Kaden taking it?"

"As well as can be expected. They're going to need someone to talk to. I'd planned on asking you for recommendations for a family and grief counselor."

Dr. Tailor scribbled a note. "I'll have Ruth Anne send you a few recommendations."

"Thanks."

"I'd like to see you on a more regular basis for the next month or so."

"Why?"

"You're coming in on an as-needed basis, which has been working for you. You found your niche and your purpose and you've been settled. But you have a lot of turmoil happening around you. We haven't discussed how you're handling Bree's issues, but I know that's probably adding a decent amount of worry and stress on top of everything else you have going on with Sarah and the kids and now a new guy." She paused. "Which means the f-word."

Denise blinked in confusion.

"Feelings, Denise."

"Oh! *That* f-word."

"Yes, that f-word." She raised her hands and made air quotes. "*Liking* this guy, means you're having feelings."

Her lip curled up in disgust and she growled low in the back of her throat. "I don't do feelings."

"You've been stingy with your feelings for the last decade, only doling them out to a very small, select group of people. Mainly your family and Bree, who you consider your family. Which is one of the reasons I want to see you more frequently for a while. You're going to be dealing with a lot of emotions and reactions you've been suppressing. I haven't pressed this issue before because you adapted in a way I felt was healthy for you, but if you get serious about this guy, it's going to bring up a lot of things you've been ignoring."

Closing her eyes, Denise took a deep, steady breath and released it slowly. Fuck. She didn't know if she was ready for this. Having everything that was going on in her life listed out just made it seem like a soup sandwich. Doc Tailor was right, though. If she didn't get a handle on everything, it would all come crashing down on her and bury her—something she'd learned the hard way in the past.

"Alright."

"Good." She made some more notes. "Set up the next four appointments with Ruth before you leave."

"Okay." She scratched Sprocket's head. *Feelings. Blech.* Bree was never going to let her live this down when she found out.

CHAPTER 12

"W hat's this one? It looks like a peacock." Chris traced the swirls of color in the partial sleeve tattoo that covered the upper half of her right arm.

"A Japanese phoenix," she said.

"When did you get it?" His fingers swept softly down her arm to her fingers.

"After about a year after I began therapy." Her own fingers followed the dark lines of the traditional American eagle tattoo that stretched across his chest. "What about this?"

"That took a few sessions to complete."

"I can imagine. The detail is fantastic. Why old-school?"

"My old man owned a tattoo shop. His expertise was old-school, Sailor Jerry tattoos. Most of his customers were military and bikers. He gave me my first tattoo." He was quiet for a moment. "He was killed during a robbery. Some junkie looking for money figured my dad would have a lot of cash in the parlor."

She pressed her lips against his pec muscle. "I'm sorry."

"Thanks. It was a long time ago."

"Do you have any other family?

"An older sister and a younger brother. You?"

"Only child, but my cousin came to live with us when I was fifteen, so she's more sister than cousin."

His hand followed the faint lines of gray on her ribcage to her back and he pressed her toward him, pulling more of her weight onto her front. "What about her?"

Even though she couldn't see it, she tried to look over her shoulder at the tattoo that took up a good portion of her back. "Joan of Arc, patron saint of soldiers and the Women's Army Corps."

"Really? I had no idea."

"I got her after we completed the CST training course."

"Appropriate. Are these smoke tendrils?"

She raised her arm, exposing the underside of her breast. "It's not supposed to be, but I can see how it looks like that. It's supposed to be wind blowing the pennant she's holding. There are scars there I wanted to cover up."

His fingers followed the ink back and he palmed her breast. "Scars from what?"

"IED blast. It detonated early, so no one was seriously injured, but I took some shrapnel between the plates of my vest."

His head came down and he sucked her nipple into his mouth, flicking it with his tongue. "I was going to say it was a really good boob job because this baby feels totally real."

That deserved a smack against the back of his head.

"Hey! It was a compliment."

She mocked glared at him, trying not to let how good his mouth felt on her show on her face. Her legs were restless and she dragged her foot against his calf.

Grinning down at her, he said, "I can see how what I said might not have been taken as a compliment."

"Do you?" God, his smile made her insides jump and twist. His playfulness, especially in bed, made him seem like a little kid at an amusement park and her body was the best ride there.

"I'm willing to learn from the error of my ways."

"Huh. How do you plan on doing that?"

He rolled onto his back, pulling her on top of him and spreading her legs so she straddled his hips, keeping them chest to chest. His hands stretched wide and smoothed up the back of her legs, to the juncture of her thighs. One of his fingers circled her slick opening, before slowing sliding in.

Her eyelids fluttered shut and she groaned.

Chris pulled her head down until their lips brushed against each other. "Allow me to demonstrate."

DENISE'S PHONE pinged on her nightstand, pulling her out of her semi-sleep. Lying on her side, she was pressed up against Chris's back, an arm draped over his waist and a leg thrown over his hips. She rolled to her back and stared at the plain, flat ceiling.

She hadn't dreamed. Or, if she had, she didn't remember it. There was always a sense of what she'd dreamed, usually helplessness or grief, even if she didn't wake up with the details. Turning her head, she looked at Chris's back. *What if* and *maybe* whispered in her head. *What if* she could be really happy? *Maybe* with someone who understood there would be times that would be difficult? Maybe it wouldn't end up being with Chris, but staring at his broad back, watching his ribs rise and fall, she felt something deep in her chest she hadn't felt in a very long time.

Hope.

Her phone pinged again and she grabbed it off the nightstand.

Bree was attacked. Air evac'd to Duke-Raleigh.

She bolted upright. "What the fuck?"

Chris shot up next to her. "What?"

Pressing the call button next to Jase's name, she kicked free of the covers and lunged across the room toward her dresser.

"Jase. What the hell?" she asked when he finally answered.

"Her assistant attacked her."

She yanked her underwear over her hips. "Cindy?" There was no way. "Quiet, nice, says 'golly-darn,' Cindy?

"Deranged, homicidal Cindy. If that's Bree's assistant, then yeah, that Cindy."

"Fuck." Shoving the phone between her ear and her shoulder, she pulled a sports bra out of a drawer. "How long ago? Is she at the hospital yet? Who found her?

"I don't know all the details yet. Tim called twenty minutes ago and said she was in critical condition and they were rushing her to Raleigh."

She yanked the bra over hear head. "What about Gran?"

"Tim called her first."

"Okay. I'm on my way." Ending the call, she threw the phone on the end of the bed and snatched a shirt and shorts out of the dresser.

"What's going on?" Chris had put on his boxers while she'd been talking to Jase.

Pulling her shirt over her head, she said, "Bree was attacked. She's being taken to Duke-Raleigh Hospital."

"Do they know who attacked her?" He sat on the bed and slid his legs into his jeans. Good to know he did it like normal folk.

"Jase said it was her assistant."

He grabbed his shirt from the floor. "You don't think so?"

She twisted her hair up into a messy bun. "I don't know. If I'd had to pick someone to be Bree's stalker, she never would have been on the list. I don't know. They always say it's the quiet ones." She braced her hands on her hips and stared at the floor, having a hard time picturing Cindy trying to attack Bree.

A deep, low whine came from the other side of her bedroom door. Shaking herself from her thoughts, she opened the door and bent to Sprocket. "I'm okay, girl. Just a little worried. We're gonna go see Bree." Sprocket licked at her chin and Denise pulled her head back out of slobber range.

"She can sense your moods from another room?" Chris asked, standing behind her.

"I guess so. She's usually not that far from me." She stood and stepped around the dog.

"How do you mean?"

"She has a bed in my room, so if I'm asleep, she's still close to me." She slid her feet into her flip-flops beside the door.

"Oh. Sorry I kicked you out of your bed."

Denise looked over her shoulder to find Chris scratching Sprocket behind the ear. It was a first. There'd never been a reason for her to close her bedroom door before. She hadn't even done it, Chris had.

Snatching her keys and wallet from the table in the entryway, she grabbed Sprocket's vest from the hook on the wall and opened the door. Sprocket went ahead of her and Chris followed her out. She locked the deadbolt and jogged down the stairs.

At the bottom of the stairs Chris wrapped his arms around her waist and pulled her close. "Hey. Hang on a sec. I know you're in a hurry. Do you want me to go with you?"

She swallowed and licked her lips. Yes. And no. The hospital wasn't the place to explain why she and Chris were together. Hell, she hadn't even had a chance to tell Bree they'd hooked up. "No. I don't know how long it's going to be. I'm sure you need to be at work tomorrow."

"Won't be the first time I've gone to work dragging ass." He tucked a loose strand of hair behind her ear.

She smiled. "It's alright." Maybe she was being ungracious, but this was all still new and unfamiliar. Her parents, Bree, and Susan were the only ones she leaned on.

And she'd never been the type to let anyone carry her burden for her anyway.

His lips were soft and firm at the same time. "I'll call you later and see how you're doing."

Deep down—way, way deep down—she could admit it felt nice that someone other than family was worried about her.

RV30

Rendezvous in thirty-minutes.

Shit. That was not the message he was expecting. Chris dropped his head onto the headrest of the drivers seat and rubbed his forehead. Damn it! He wanted to call Denise and let her know, but protocol dictated he cease all unencrypted communication and make his way to the rendezvous point.

He gripped the steering wheel until his knuckles turned white and growled deep in his throat. Fuck. Powering down his phone, he threw it onto the passenger seat and took a deep breath.

He had to trust Denise would understand when he got the chance to fill her in. If Phil was at the rendezvous point, he'd make sure he passed a message to Denise—let her know what was going on and that he'd contact her as soon as he got back from this op.

Whenever that was.

CHAPTER 13

*D*enise checked her phone one more time before slipping it into her pocket. She eased into Bree's hospital room.

"Jase," she hissed. "The nurses are going to lose their shit if they see you in bed with her."

"Then guard the door. And quit yelling."

"Why're you in bed with her?"

"She woke up. Got upset when I told her about whack job."

Bree opened her eyes. "Don't call her that."

Jase peered down his nose. "You fakin'?"

"Just woke up."

Denise poked him in the ribs. "Get out. My turn." She held his stare for several moments. He was not going to win this argument, even if it was silent. She needed time with her best friend.

He sighed and rolled out of the bed. Turning, he leaned down and brushed Bree's hair back from her face. "Careful of her arm."

"No shit." Denise pushed him out of the way and crawled up on the bed. Grasping Bree's fingers, she moved her arm onto her chest and lay down facing her. "How're you feeling?"

"Weak."

"That'll happen when you lose most of your blood."

"Is there water?"

She looked over her shoulder, but Jase already had the cup ready. He angled the straw so Bree could drink. When she was finished, he walked around the end of the bed and sat next to Bree's legs.

"What's the rule?" Denise demanded.

Bree shook her head.

"Don't take stupid chances."

"Didn't have much of a choice. She was in my house when I got home."

She touched her forehead to Bree's. "You scared me," she whispered. "Don't do it again." She'd never been so worried in her life. Not even when Susan had received her diagnosis. Maybe because she'd had time to come to terms with the news, but Bree's attack had shaken her to her core.

"Agreed."

"What do y'all think you're doin'?"

Denise craned her neck to look over her shoulder. Nurse Mary Ann stood in the doorway, hands on her hips. "Get off that poor girl." She stormed forward and waved her hand at Jase, as if shooing away a fly, and smacked Denise on the leg. "Off. Bad enough someone tried to fillet her like a fish, she doesn't need y'all piling on top of her."

Denise rolled off the edge of the bed and pulled her phone from her back pocket, shooting a text to Gran to let her know Bree was awake.

"You look like crap," Bree told Jase.

Denise huffed out a short laugh. "I told him to go home and take a shower." He'd refused. She'd finally relented and driven out to his house to grab him some clean clothes. Thankfully, Bree's room had a shower so he hadn't been able to build up any manly funk. She had enough issues with hospital smell.

"He wouldn't leave your side," Mary Ann added. "Called in the big guns when we tried to kick him out."

"Big guns?" Bree asked.

"Gran," Jase said.

"Where is she?"

"She's coming back this evening," Jase said.

Denise stepped out of Mary Ann's way when she left to get more bandages, then sat in the chair close to the door. "I sent her a text to let her know you were awake. She'll be here soon."

"How long have I been here?" Bree asked.

"Three days," she said.

"Three days?" Bree's head rose from the flat pillow, but dropped again immediately.

"How much do you remember?" Jase asked.

"All of it. Right up until Tim and Detective Johnson stormed in. How's Katherine?"

"She was stabbed twice in the stomach," Denise said. "I think the doctors had to remove a kidney, but she's conscious. They have her a couple rooms down the hall."

"I'd like to go see her when I can," Bree said.

Jase crossed his arms. "I'll wheel you down when the doctor says you can move around."

Bree glared. "My arm is cut, not my leg."

"Did Cindy—?" Mary Ann's arrival cut her off before she could ask whether Cindy had told Bree why she went whack-a-doodle. After the nurse, it was the doctor, then Detective Johnson came in. He asked Bree all the questions Denise had rattling in her brain.

Jesus. It all came down to a guy. She could see how much Cindy's break was affecting Bree, though. Tears welled up from her tightly closed eyes and rolled down her face.

Fuck the nurses. They could try to kick her out of Bree's room. Jase moved up the bed and leaned over Bree, and Denise lay down in the bed again, carefully wrapping her arm around her. After a few moments, she wiped some of Bree's tears away.

"Just think of all the new stuff you'll have to talk to Dr. Tailor about. She's probably sick of hearing about the same old shit.

Bree snorted and blew out a snot bubble.

Denise threw back her head and laughed, almost rolling herself off the bed.

"Get me a tissue, you cow."

It was probably a good thing Bree couldn't use her arm, because she would have pushed Denise off the bed if she'd been able. Bree blew her nose with a tissue Jase handed her.

The detective left, telling Bree he would likely have more questions later. Her yawn was so huge, Denise was surprised her jaw didn't pop.

"I'm going to head out," she said. "Gran texted while you were talking to the detective. She'll be here around two. Plenty of time to take a nap."

"Okay."

She laid her forehead against Bree's again. "I'm glad you're safe."

"Me, too."

She kissed Bree's cheek and eased out of the bed. "Later, Jase."

Eavesdropping was bad, but she couldn't help letting the door close slowly to watch her best friend and her man.

"I love you," he said. "Snot bubbles and all. You can't ever leave me, Bree. For..."

Shit. That was too personal. She had a sudden desire to talk to Chris.

Pulling her phone from her back pocket, she unlocked the screen. Still no missed calls or texts. She stopped in the middle of the hall.

"Ma'am?"

Glancing over her shoulder, she saw she'd stopped right in front of a nurse pushing a patient in a wheelchair.

"Sorry." She stepped out of the way. Jeez, her situational awareness was shit at the moment.

He hadn't called or sent her a text. It'd been days since Bree's attack. Had he said for her to call or that he'd call? Was this the three day rule?

She shook her head. No. That wasn't his style. He'd never been shy about being in her space. But...not even a text?

Glancing up, she made sure her path to the elevator was unobstructed, then let her thumbs fly across the screen. She hit send as she reached the elevator bank.

Message undeliverable

Stupid hospitals. Bree had told her the surgeons at Fort Bragg used old style flip phones as their on-call phones because of the shielding in the hospital. She exited the elevators and tried to send the text again as soon as she cleared the exterior doors.

Message undeliverable

Her brow furrowed. She had five dots now that she was out of the hospital. She pressed the call button and pressed the phone to her ear.

"The number you have dialed is no longer in service."

What the hell? Staring at the phone in her hand, she tried again. Same message.

What. The. Fuck. She shook her head and stalked to her SUV. Wrenching the door open, she climbed in and slammed the door shut.

Think rationally. Don't let the crazy chick take over. Because that bitch wanted to drive over to his house and pound on the door until he answered, then kick him in the nuts before demanding an explanation for why he hadn't called her like he said and then dropped off the face of the earth.

Not caring to look too closely at her reaction to the situation, she started the SUV and pulled out of the parking spot. She worked on calming her breathing and the heart that felt like it was trying to hammer its way out of her rib cage.

There was a reason. It might suck, but there was always a reason.

~

DENISE PULLED to the curb in front of Bree's house, shifted to neutral, and set the brake. She rested her head on the steering wheel and fought the urge to go back home. Bree was expecting her and Denise was running out of excuses. Bree was also getting suspicious of Denise's excuses and had all but threatened to have Jase drive her to Denise's if she didn't haul her butt over.

Four days since she'd learned Chris's phone had been disconnected. Three days of beating back the urge to find him, chase him down, and demand to know why. Two days of feeling like someone had tied a lead balloon to something inside her that dragged her down and made it hard to move.

Sprocket whined and pressed her cold nose against Denise's cheek. She cringed at the feeling of slobber on her cheek and scratched her dog under the chin. "I'll be okay. It's what we do."

She turned off the engine and held the door open while Sprocket jumped down. Trudging up the yard to the side of the house, she tried to fluff up her happy before she went inside. Bree would see right through her, so she had to at least put in a good effort at faking it. No sense in upsetting Bree with everything she'd just been through.

"Honey...I'm home!" She hung her keys on the hook by the door and kicked off her sandals under the bench in the mud room then made her way into the kitchen. Charlie trotted around the corner to greet Sprocket, his butt wagging non-stop. "Anyone here?"

"We're in the living room," Bree called.

"I'm going to grab some tea, do you need anything?"

"We're good," Bree said, crossing the threshold from the living room. She was still a little pale, dark circles prominent under her eyes.

"Shouldn't you be resting?" Denise asked.

"My arm was cut. I wasn't struck by lightning."

Hello, belligerence. "I take it Jase wants you to rest more?"

"I threatened to punch him in the balls again." She cocked a hip and rested it against the counter. "Told him it wouldn't matter to me since he wasn't letting me play with them anyway."

The last bit of cold tea she was swallowing shot up her nose and she coughed. She set her cup on the counter and stuck her fingers in her ears. "La la la la la. I don't need that visual."

"Well, you've got it. Why have you been avoiding me?"

"I've been avoiding everyone, not just you."

"Why?"

She returned the pitcher of tea to the fridge. "Why're you so crabby?"

"I've moved onto anger. I can't take it out on Cindy, so I'm taking it out on the people I love. It's healthy. You should try it."

Denise leaned back against the counter and crossed her arms. "I'll keep that in mind when I get there."

"But there's something going on for you to get there?"

She gave her best friend a curt nod.

"Hmm." Bree turned back to the living room.

Denise rolled her eyes to the ceiling and huffed out a breath. Bree didn't get like that very often, but when she did no one was safe. If she didn't think Bree would keep poking at her, she'd be so proud. She grabbed her glass and followed her friend.

Jase was sprawled on one end of the sectional, eyes fixed to a football game. "Hey, Jase."

"Hey."

At the next commercial break, Jase rose from the couch and handed the remote to Bree with a kiss. "I'll start the grill."

"Why don't you call Chris, see if he wants to come hang out."

Denise froze and slowly cut her eyes to Bree, who gave her a calculating look. That wench. Bree's eyes widened ever so slightly and Denise knew she'd figured out something had happened between them.

I can't believe you didn't tell me, she mouthed.

Hello! You got stabbed, Denise mouthed back.

Bree shot her a death glare and Denise stuck out her tongue.

"Can't," Jase said. "His phone's deactivated."

That got Bree's attention. "What do you mean his phone's deactivated?"

"It's happened a couple of times before."

"Why?" Bree asked.

Denise smiled, watching Bree get worked up on her behalf. She didn't even know the full story and she was already outraged.

"It happens when he goes deep undercover. They basically cut off any and all communication with their normal lives."

Without telling anyone?

"What about the guys with families?" Bree asked. "They just disappear without telling their spouse or kids?"

Jase came back in from the kitchen. "I don't know, babe. I've never asked him how it works."

"Well, did he tell you he was going undercover?"

"It's a guess, since his partner called me and asked me to pick up his truck for him, and that's what happened last time."

So there had been a way to get word to someone. To her, if she'd been someone important enough. Just a quick note or message letting her know he was okay and hadn't blown her off after getting in her pants. Guess she should have known better. Once again, someone's job was more of a priority than she was.

Suck it up, buttercup. At least this time no one died because of it. She still hated feeling like a chump. Stupid fucking emotions.

Sprocket rose on her hind legs, put her paws on Denise's thighs, and shoved her snout under her chin. She nudged her dog's head to the side and stared up at the ceiling.

"Denise?"

Lifting her head, she saw the concern on Bree's face.

She pressed her lips together in a parody of a smile."Later, Bree." She didn't want to share just then, with Jase on the back deck. She would. After she'd had some time to gather the pieces of her heart back together. It wasn't shattered. It wasn't even broken. *Even a half-broke heart is still broken.* She shoved that thought to the deepest, darkest corner of her mind. She refused to allow someone to have that kind of power over her again.

But it still hurt. And it was time to lock that shit down for good.

KEEP READING for an unedited sneak peek of Locked-Down Heart.

Not a fan of sneak peeks, but still want to know when the next book is coming? Sign up for Tarina's newsletter or follow her on social media: Facebook, Twitter, Instagram, Amazon, and Bookbub.

ACKNOWLEDGMENTS

Thank you to everyone who invested time and energy into making this little tidbit of Denise and Chris so much better.

To my wonderful beta team: Tami, Vicky, and Mary. Thank you so much for your input and suggestions.

Toni: Even though you aren't an author, you're more of a critique partner than a beta reader. Here's to many more lines in the future. Hopefully not too many of them in Scotland.

My wonderful editor Jessica who managed to squeeze work in before and after Retreat.

To my family and friends for your support and encouragement.

And finally to the early fans. If you're reading this, that's you. Thank you so much for the reviews, the emails, and the private messages. Your encouragement and support means so much.

ALSO BY TARINA DEATON

THE COMBAT HEART SERIES

Stitched Up Heart (Combat Hearts #1)

As an Air Force medic, Bree Marks saw the worst the War on Terror had to dish out. Now a physical therapist, she uses her experience to help other veterans heal from their physical wounds; while she battles her own emotional damage.

Blaming himself for his best friend's suicide, former Army Ranger Jase Larken, retreated from life. To honor his best friend's memory and assuage his guilt, he started an outdoor adventure company to help veterans with PTSD.

Bree had better things to do than catch her cheating fiance in bed with another woman. Jase is something better - for a night at least. For the first time in years, Jase wanted more. When he finds her again, he doesn't give her another chance to run.

Jase's protectiveness grates on Bree's independent nature. She's dealt with her fair share of alpha-male, door kickers and doesn't need one telling her what to do now. But as a new danger emerges, Bree and Jase must face their pasts, before someone's obsession with Bree destroys any chance they have of a future.

Half-Broke Heart (Combat Hearts #1.5)

Denise Reynolds is used to putting up a good front to show the world a strong, capable woman, but keeps a lot of things buried deep.

Chris Nolton is everything she learned the hard way to avoid — a sexy alpha-male who could charm her out of her pants and work his way into her heart. If history has taught her anything, it's a deadly combination, but he manages to dig up emotions and longing she's tried to bury for years.

He says all the right things and pushes her boundaries in all the right ways. Letting her guard down is difficult, especially since believing all the right things in the past led to unimaginable consequences.

Being content with her life may no longer be an option, but risking her heart may bring her to her knees.

Author's Note: Half-Broke Heart picks up in the middle of Stitched Up Heart (Combat Hearts #1) and is not intended to be read as a standalone.

Locked-Down Heart (Combat Hearts #2)

Denise Reynolds's tightly controlled life is thrown off kilter when she's given custody of her young cousins. There are days she has a hard enough time getting herself out of bed, never mind two precocious kids.

If that wasn't enough, Chris Nolton comes strolling back into town as suddenly as he left it. She'd broken her own rules and given him a chance once before, only to have him ghost on her. But he's not there for her this time. No, he's leading the FBI Task Force intent on capturing the kids' biological father. A man who was sent to prison for manslaughter. A man who was released five years too early. A man who wants his kids back.

The past has a way of repeating itself and once again, Denise finds herself defending the innocent against the evil of world. One wrong decision, one second guess, could have devastating consequences. To protect the most important people in her life, she'll need to trust the one man with the power to break her.

Rescued Heart (Combat Hearts #3)

From New York Times best-selling author Cristin Harber and Tarina Deaton comes an exciting collaboration…

"Please, Jordan. It's Emme."

The last thing Major Jordan Grant expected was to be pulled off his unit's deployment for a civilian mission. But when Titan calls, you answer — especially when the mission is to rescue the younger sister of your childhood best friend.

Moments away from death, NGO nurse Emme France could only pray for a miracle. The last person she expected to see in the smoke and dust was Jordan Grant, her teenage crush and litmus test of all the men she'd dated ever since.

Lying low at Titan's exotic Abu Dhabi headquarters while the media furor around her rescue settles, Emme and Jordan explore a mutual attraction that is no longer young and innocent. Days in the desert paradise ignite desire and blur reality...until they return home, where Jordan rejoins his deployed unit and Emme is left alone to reevaluate her life and priorities.

Their passion was forged in the fires of combat. Will the home fires be enough to keep the burn alive?

LOCKED-DOWN HEART

Chapter One

Boom. Boom. Boom.

Denise woke with a start. Rolling off the edge of the bed, she took up a defensive position. Heart pounding, she crouched in the small space between the bed and wall and reached for her gun, groping in the dim light. Where the fuck was her gun?

A groan sounded from the bed and sheets rustled. The jangle of dog tags worked it's way into her consciousness as she came fully awake. Sprocket, her 200-pound English Mastiff, eased herself off the bed and stuck her snout in Denise's face, bathing her with doggie breath and smearing slobber on her cheek.

"Ugh, quit that." Denise pushed her dog's huge head away and wiped her face with the sleeve of her worn t-shirt. "I'm awake." Sprocket huffed at her.

The pounding came again. The door. The luminous numbers on the clock showed four-twenty-three. Shit, she'd fallen asleep. Who the hell was at the pounding at the door? She reached between the mattress and the boxspring for her Glock.

"Come on." Pushing at Sprocket, she rose from her position on the floor and followed the dog out the room.

Kimber stood in the door of her and Kaden's bedroom. Denise shifted her hand behind her back.

"Who is it, Aunt Denny?"

"I don't know sweetheart. I'm going to check. Sorry I fell asleep."

"It's okay. You've had a hard week."

Not something a nine-year-old should be worrying about. "How's your homework going?"

She shrugged. "I'm done. I've been helping Kaden with his."

"Okay. We'll sit down and go over yours after I see who's at the door."

Kimber put a hand on Sprocket. "Can Sprocket stay here?"

"Sure. Looking at the dog, she said, "Stay with K-Squared." Sprocket sat and licked her chops. "Good girl."

Holding the gun low beside her leg, finger poised along the trigger guard, she walked through the small, combined living room and dining room. She glanced through the peephole, then rocked back on her heels.

What the fuck? She stared at the door, trying to decide if she should open it or not.

Three more sharp knocks made the decision for her.

She unlocked the door and yanked it open.

"What the hell are you doing here?" she demanded.

Chris took a step back. Whether from the door opening suddenly, her, or her question, she wasn't sure. *He looks tired.* It wasn't her problem. Never was.

"Denise?"

"Yes, Chris. What are you doing here?"

The lines between his dark eyebrows grew more pronounced. "What are *you* doing here?"

His strong jaw was covered with stubble, accentuating the lines of his mouth. A mouth that was surprisingly soft, especially when it grazed over her skin. Her nipples pebbled under her thin t-shirt. Damn her traitorous body. It'd been almost four months, it should have gotten the message by now.

"I asked first." She set her gun on the high shelf above the coat hooks and grabbed the zip-up hoodie hanging by the door.

"Why are you answering the door with a gun?" he asked.

"Because this isn't the greatest neighborhood." The neighborhood sucked. It wasn't the greatest when her cousin bought the small three-bedroom house and it had only gone down in the last five years. She was pretty sure her neighbor two doors down was dealing. As long as he wasn't cooking, and he kept it to his doorstep, she was willing to over look it. But Kimber and Kaden were going to her parents' the minute the school year was over.

"Why are you here?" She enunciated the question this time. She needed a quick answer so she could work on forgetting Christopher Nolton.

"I'm looking for Sarah Reed."

Her shoulders sagged and she rubbed a hand over her eyes. "She's not here."

"When will she be back?"

Denise glanced over her shoulder. Sprocket sat in the opening of the short hall that led to the two small bedrooms at the back of the house. She let out a low woof and laid down, resting her head on her paws. Denise stepped out of the house and pulled the door shut behind her, leaving it cracked. Chris stepped back on the small concrete pad.

"She's not coming back. She's in the hospital with terminal cancer."

Light dawned behind his eyes. "Shit. She's your cousin." Chris ran his hands over his hair. Hair that had grown long in the last three months and now curled around his ears and jawline.

She crossed her arms over her chest. "What is this about?"

He took a deep breath. "Her ex-husband was released from prison. He skipped parole."

She dropped her arms. "What the fuck? He's not supposed to be out for another five years. At least."

His face pinched, like he had sucked on something sour. "He made a good impression with the parole board. Got out early. I need to know why her ex has been calling her."

"What? He hasn't been calling her."

"Denise, he's been contacting her. We traced the calls to this residence."

Anger threatened to strangle her. "I will guran-damn-tee you, she hasn't had any contact with that fuckwad in almost ten years."

"Aunt Denny? What's going on?" Kaden stood in the doorway behind them.

She took a deep breath and schooled her features. "Hey, buddy. What are you doing?"

"I heard talking." He pointed at Chris. "Who's he?"

"Just a friend," she said. She brushed his hair back from his forehead. "Why don't you go back inside? I'll be there in a few minutes and we can read before dinner.

"Is Mom okay?"

"She's fine. We're still going to go see her Friday after school."

Kaden stared at Chris, eyeing him from top to bottom. He looked between them before asking, "Is this about the man that's been calling?"

"What man?" Denise glanced at Chris, trying to gage his reaction. He stared intently at Kaden, but didn't ask any questions.

"He said he's our dad, but Mom said he was dead. He keeps asking to talk to Mom." He dropped his head and looked down at his toes. "Am I in trouble for talking to him?"

"Hey. No." She grasped his chin and turned his face toward her. "You're not in trouble. I'll explain everything later, okay? I don't want you to worry about anything."

His gaze was too serious, too somber for a eight-year-old little boy who shouldn't have any cares in the world.

"Go back inside. I'll be in there in a minute." She kissed his forehead and turned him by his shoulders. "Go with Sprocket." She watched as he walked back into the house, hanging onto her dog's neck.

She leaned against the door jam facing Chris. "That answers that question."

"You need to warn him," he said, pointing through the open doorway.

She glanced over her shoulder to make sure Kaden wasn't in sight and spoke in a low voice. "I know. I don't know why Eddie's calling here all of a sudden. That fuckwit hasn't shown any interest in his kids since they were conceived. Why are you involved in this?"

He shoved his hands in the pocket of his jeans pushing them a tad bit further down his lean hips. "I've been assigned to this case."

She blinked. "What case? Assigned how?"

"FBI, remember?"

"So?"

He looked off to the side and took a deep breath, letting it out through his nose. "I'm on a violent gang task force."

Understanding dawned. "Eddie was a member of the Southern Anarchists."

"Yeah."

She scrubbed her hands over her face. "I'll disconnect the phone tomorrow."

"We don't actually want you do that."

She dropped her hands and stared at him. "I don't give a shit what you want. He's not having any contact with those kids."

"Denise, this is one of the few links we have to the Anarchists. We need it. Just warn the kids not to give him any information when they talk to him."

"Let me say it again. I don't give a flying fuck. And you're sure as shit not using those kids as bait or as a way in to a criminal gang. It's going to be a moot point in a few weeks anyway when I move them out of this house."

"Denise—"

"No. I'm not putting those kids in the middle of a war between the FBI and the Anarchists. I'll do what I need to do to protect them. End of story."

She stepped back into the house and closed the door firmly. She wanted to slam it, but didn't want to upset the kids. How dare he? Who the hell did he think he was to show up after disappearing into thin air and ask her to use her cousins as a connection to a damn gang.

Jesus. She needed to talk to Sarah.

ABOUT THE AUTHOR

Tarina has spent her entire life in and around the military - first as a dependent and then as an enlisted Air Force member.

A life-long day-dreamer, she never envisioned being a published author was a possibility. All that changed when a friend challenged her to complete NaNoWriMo. She dusted off one of the many stories she had started over the years, threw it in the trash, and started all over.

Her debut novel, Stitched Up Heart, released in September 2016. She draws heavily from her own military experience to create authentic characters and challenges.

Tarina is still active duty and a single mom of young twins. Her favorite hobby is sleep. She has delusions of retiring from the military and being a stay-at-home mom.

Sign up for Tarina's newsletter: http://eepurl.com/b3ABd1
www.tarinadeaton.com
tarina.deaton@tarinadeaton.com